DEADLINE

Also by Tom Stacey:

The Worm in the Rose

DEADLINE

TOM STACEY

St. Martin's Press
New York

Library of Congress Cataloging-in-Publication Data

Stacey, Tom.
      Deadline / Tom Stacey.
          p.   cm.
      "A Thomas Dunne book."
      ISBN 0-312-03320-6
      I. Title.
PR6069.T18D4   1989
813'.54—dc20   89-34861
                                                                CIP

First published in Great Britain by William Heinemann Ltd.

First U.S. Edition

10 9 8 7 6 5 4 3 2 1

Dedication

My Dear Ralph

By asking leave to dedicate this story to you, I am acknow-
ledging what it owes to you: it would not come to have been
written had you not been living where you were when you
were. Gran Jones is of course not Ralph Izzard. You did not go
to live in your Gulf island because of any distant love affair;
you were never neglected by yourself or forgotten by your
friends; your house was invariably a welcoming place, and a
famous haven for those of us to whom you would surrender
your spare bedroom; you have always been treasured by your
family; you were never crusty or curmudgeonly. And far from
resenting the younger bloods of your vocation, you were a
source of affection and inspiration.

You were (and are) one of the surviving mythic figures of the
old-time Fleet Street, in which each of us grew up a generation
apart. In that respect you resemble Gran Jones. And I somehow
feel that if a *putsch* had occurred on your chosen island, your
professional daemon would have taken over in some such way
as Gran Jones's. You would have set aside every consideration
except getting to the core of it all and then moving your copy
(as we would say) come hell or high water or, if need be, heaven.
So I have borrowed that from you, as I have borrowed your car,
your parrot and the architecture of your home.

All else I have made out of the dust of years of travelling and
foreign corresponding – the old Emir and his tricky son, those
pushy young newsmen, Al Bakr the ageing revolutionary, my
sturdy seamen Nasir and Ismail, well-meaning Williams. And
Romy – ah, Romy . . . All to tell the tale of a man of whom in the
end it seemed nothing was left: nothing, that is, except his
consuming *métier*.

Yours ever

Tom

1

Friday was the day of rest, and since it was a Friday, and not
long before lunch, Gran Jones drifted into the bar-room of the
Darwish Hotel with his unopened mail and copies of the
Morning Post in their blue airmail wrappers, and settled his
spent and lofty frame into one of the deep chairs by the long
window. He wouldn't have long to wait for Abdullah to bring
him what Abdullah had brought him at midday on a Friday for
years. Viewed from the window, the only blemish on the
shallow Gulf's mottled aquamarine was the distant speckling
of oil rigs. It was all quite normal, you might even say serene. It
was years since he'd wished for anything out of the ordinary. It
was probably quite a while since he had looked for it. He knew
that wasn't a professional attitude for a journalist, but he wasn't
going to let that bother him. He was all but done up, an old
man now, and a dessicated pattern of existence was the right of
old men. Who was there to tell him different?

He frowned across at the bunch of fellow expatriates at the
bar. Wasn't it rather more crowded than usual?

He might be taciturn, but wasn't a cold man. Regulars from
the island's British community would usually greet him from
the bar with a nod or a little wave, and those who knew him
well might wander over to his table. He would down his first
Tuborg before opening his mail, the worthless stuff first . . . not
that the rest of it would contain anything of consequence. Once
a week was often enough to collect this kind of mail. Any
companions so far gathered would chat among themselves as
he scanned his correspondence, which he held at arm's length
since for at least ten years now he had put off getting new
glasses. After the tedious letters he broke the wrappers of the
Post with a loose-skinned, half-crouched finger. Opening up a
newspaper was still a pleasure.

As a rule he would sip his Tuborg until about two o'clock,

I

then consume a small helping of the curry or meat pie the Darwish served in the bar on Fridays. For a big-framed man he ate little. There was no flesh on him. He would linger on until about three or four with his coffee and a cigar, depending on who there was to talk to. Then he would gather up his copies of the *Post* and the letters, leaving the wrappers and the envelopes for Abdullah to clear away. He would climb into his twenty-year-old white Packard which had had trouble with its silencer for as long as his friends could remember, and drive back very slowly through the modern part of town into what was left of the warren of the old town, where he lived.

Jones had always used the Darwish's post-box as his own. When he had first come to live on the island, the Darwish was the only hotel, apart from a few Arab doss-houses. When wealth struck the island, devastating nine tenths of what the place had once been, other locally financed amateurish hotels sprang up like rank weeds and made quick easy money. The Darwish met the challenge first by attempting to air-condition its spacious airy rooms (a futile endeavour), and then with a great heave-ho and at a scrambling pace rebuilt itself on its own site grandly. They even rewrote the lunch and dinner menus in Egyptian-flavoured American restaurant rodomontade. For a while it held on to its reputation as the only hotel of quality. Then up went the Sheraton and Hilton and Holiday Inn and Ramada Palace. The Darwish settled for the old Gulf hands, the discerning, those who liked to suppose their visits to the island were prompted by more than mere avarice – actual fondness for the place, for instance, a nostalgic British allegiance to it. The Darwish kept its staff, knew its customers, and allowed its *habitués* credit.

'When camels are browsing in the foyer of the Hilton,' Jones had been heard to comment, 'the Darwish will still be in business.' Jones had authority to engage in this kind of prophecy among the expatriates since such venerable age, which reached indefinitely back to before the present era of the island's history, seemed to reach indefinitely forward also. It seemed plausible that Jones himself would still be found in the Darwish in this future epoch of Hilton-browsing camels, and his own bar account still overdue.

2

Few who patronised the Darwish did not know Gran Jones, and vitually every permanent resident of the island, native and expatriate alike, knew *of* him. The Arab tongue has difficulty with the elision of certain consonants, and many an island Arab called him Jonas, which would often slide into the Islamic name Yunus. This Jonas or Yunus was known by virtue of having lived on the island longer than any other Westerner, and – in a Western way – for his unrivalled knowledge. As for those Westerners who came and went, whether on visits of two or three weeks, or two or three years, they would advise each other sagely to 'have a word with Gran Jones: he knows everything'. They would turn up at the Darwish bar on a Friday especially to consult him; for the price of a round of drinks they picked up what they needed – perhaps the name of an official with influence in this or that department of government, or which booth in the old suk still dealt in brass-bound Gulf chests.

These last several years so much money had been around that if Jones had been rewarded with, say, one per cent of the profit resulting from the knowledge he gratuitously disbursed, he would have been a rich man. But he had no interest in money and consequently no knack of making it. Amid a community of extraordinary wealth, amid profligacy that was often flagrant, Jones remained perilously poor.

His only regular income came from retainer fees provided from London's *The Morning Post* and an American political weekly as their local stringer. The island's oil wealth made the place significant, but it seldom produced news and for years the Emir had pursued a policy of keeping the island and himself out of the news. In this policy the Emir had been advised by Jones – advice which was against Jones's own financial interest since only by being asked for a dispatch, or by volunteering one which was published, could he supplement his paltry retainer fees. His single undisputed skill was that of a newspaperman. In his time he had been one of the most celebrated of his profession, not just in the Gulf or even in the Middle East, but as a worldwide roving correspondent for the selfsame *Morning Post*.

3

So the island did not warrant staff correspondents, and, once having made the bizarre decision to settle in the Gulf, Jones could earn his living only as a freelance. Widely known staff reporters breezed in from time to time, when the price of oil got jumpy, or political realignment threatened the fragile equilibrium of the region, or an American Secretary of State stopped over on a courtesy call. These visiting newsmen would pick Jones's brains over a few glasses of Tuborg; they might obtain an interview with one of Emir's ministers; after a night or two at the Darwish (which had a reputation among newspapermen) they would file their twelve hundred words or make their little broadcasts, and, grousing about the lack of press facilities, fly out.

Although the value of his sterling retainer retainer fees had shrunk to a third of their original worth, Jones hadn't dared ask for an increase for years now, lest his semi-masters decided to make his plea an excuse to hire some young newshound from the local English-language paper in his place. He could envisage a role for a busy young journalist who could cover the whole Gulf from the island and string for half the principal journals and broadcast networks of the English-speaking world. Such a fellow could blank him out, take the last bread from his mouth. And then what? He hadn't saved anything, there was no pension secretly accumulating, no country cottage in Dorset . . . As it was, only one of the news agencies, Associated Press, had got around to appointing their own stringer on the island. Young McCulloch didn't constitute a threat. For one thing, as editor of the local English daily, McCulloch couldn't put his resident's permit at risk by stirring things up; and, for another, wire services like AP didn't expect their stringer to dig for news.

Not that one had had to dig, lately. It was common knowledge that the Emir's younger son Hatim, after two years at a quite small, new, English university not yet numbered with Oxford and Cambridge, was now under house arrest in a princely villa and had grown to become, however improbably, a kind of figurehead for supporters of the regional underground 'liberation' movement, for which the island was the clandestine base. The elder son, considered feeble, was occupied with a

4

seemingly unending course of general instruction at a Texan university. Neither had been named heir apparent. For succession not to be resolved in one of the world's richest states (in capital reserves) was an unsettling factor in the affairs of the region.

Jones loved the island too much to poke around for trouble. The old Emir was a despot but a benign and respected one, a sight more trustworthy than any populist junta clinging to power with the usual Newspeak and a secret police. What was there to suppose the thinly schooled youth Hatim knew what he was playing with? In any case publicity would nourish the mischievous pretensions of his 'supporters'. Jones saw no purpose in providing it. Consequently, of symptoms of unrest he reported the minimum. The island came before his income. The old Emir, for his part, although not his landlord, somehow saw to it that the rent Jones paid for his house had not risen as all other property rentals on the island had risen. The old ruler always gave thought to detail.

Jones occupied one of the merchant houses built in the last century, when pearling flourished. It had been a gem of its kind. Jones's portion of this extensive family compound was complete in itself, with a wind tower to funnel down into the elegantly long main room, the *majlis*, the lightest breeze during the sweltering summer months. Two little bedrooms and a bathroom formed a right-angle with the kitchen and the *majlis*, and all the rooms looked inward upon a narrow patio, where a green parrot presided, and a narrow garden. A high coral wall abruptly terminated Jones's share of garden; the other part, unseen save for the tops of its two date-palms, belonged to the main dwelling which completed the original inward-gathered family compound. There resided Jones's landlord, an ageing scion of a former pearling family, a man now grown rich again in the frenzy of construction, some of which had taken place on land of which his shaky claims to ownership the Emir had endorsed.

Today this part of the town was neglected and half abandoned. Litter and rubble cluttered the alleys. Jones's house missed its annual coat of paint for several years in succession because he could not afford it. The wind tower, blocked off from the *majlis* years before when the air-conditioners were driven into the wall, was beginning to crumble. Within the house, fine dust lay deep. In a perpetual masque of life and death, lizards stalked flies all over the inner walls. Ants occupied the kitchen cupboard and sideboard; the run-off pipe of the sink was broken and released washing-up water on to the floor where morsels of food fattened a tribe of cockroaches. The kitchen was pervaded by an ineradicable odour of decay. In the *majlis*, littered with newspapers, books and archaeological bric-a-brac, the air-conditioner shuddered with such a racket that it was impossible to hear the telephone, which was installed in Jones's bedroom across the corner of the little court. He meant to have an extra bell put in the *majlis*, but that would add to his quarterly bill. In any case, around midday he usually put in a call to young McCulloch at the local paper.

Very few visited Jones. Only a handful knew exactly where he lived, and seldom nowadays did any have the occasion to enter the old quarter. The streets were awkward for cars, and the oil town lay on the other side of the capital.

For six days a week Jones was rarely seen, unless some feature article had been asked of him that got him out and about. The familiar lofty figure in crumpled canvas hat, old-fashioned denim shirt with buttoned sleeves and colonial shorts and sandals, would appear only at the local shop for a few days' provisions and seed for the parrot. Every day a borrowed servant, Aziz, lean and wheezy, a poor relation of Jones's neighbour-landlord, would step round from the adjoining house to make his bed, put the bathroom in order and run water over the dishes of the previous evening's meal which the ants had half cleaned. For six days a week Jones would stick to his own patch, waking early, rising late. At 7 a.m. he listened to the World Service of the BBC; at 7.15 a.m. he listened to the local news in English. His Arabic was not quite up to understanding the news in the language of the country: as a young man he had learned German, and one extra language would have to do. In bed in the morning he read back through all of the airmailed copies of the *Post* he collected weekly from the Darwish, except the arts reviews, the religious column, and the stock market reports. He considered it his work. A newsman must know what was going on in the world. How else might he get into proportion any news he might be called upon to file?

At about nine in the morning he would shuffle down the dark passage to the outer door in his flip-flops and sarong to pick up his copy of the local English-language daily, edited by McCulloch. He opened the parrot's cage and while his coffee was boiling he changed the sand in the tray. Then he took the parrot out on his finger and brought it with the coffee to his bedroom where he got back into bed and read. After all, it was still only just after six o'clock in London, and the middle of the night in New York. If anything broke during the daytime, Jones had three hours in hand. The first edition of the *Post* went to press around 7 p.m. London time, which was 10 p.m. local time. He knew the island's telegraphists in person. He knew the international exchange operators in person. He could move a dispatch faster than anyone on the island. He kept the telephone in his bedroom because, he reasoned, if London were to call, the time differential would most likely mean he was taking his siesta, which occupied quite a proportion of the afternoon. (New York never telephoned.)

Most of the books he read were about the Second World War and the rise of Nazi power. Modern historians kept getting things slightly wrong – played up the wrong events, drew the wrong conclusions. He himself had known many of the major players of that prolonged drama. How much vaster an affair that was than anything that had since taken place. And how the world had *shrunk*! How paltry its crises! He had known Hitler personally; twice he had interviewed him alone. As a young reporter he had walked two paces behind Hitler into the blazing Reichstag. Once Hitler himself had come on the line to him, in his flat in Berlin, to ask him in strict confidence, as 'one who understands what we are striving for in the new Reich' (Jones was then engaged to a Berlin girl: the *alliance* did not survive the outbreak of war), how the British would react to Ribbentrop's mission to London to discuss the Polish 'problem'.

He knew them all: Wavell, the Auk, Monty, Ike, Patton, Churchill, Eden, Smuts, Menzies, FDR, Truman, Attlee, Cripps, Nehru, Gandhi, Mountbatten, MacArthur. He was at Tehran and Potsdam, he covered the opening of the United Nations in San Francisco. He was not yet forty when the war was over, and one of the three or four leading newspapermen in the English-speaking world. He covered all the big post-war crises – Abadan, Korea, Berlin again, Hungary; he was the first Western reporter to tour the Soviet Union and one of only two to interview Khrushchev in the Kremlin.

By fifty, what could he add to his achievements but pallid repetitions of a greater past? He was already tired of fame, and something had gone from the centre of him. He craved privacy, and perhaps some deeply precious personal secret.

Beside his bed stood two photographs. The framed one was of his sons on a yacht, taken in the Gulf soon after he first arrived here. They were already young men then. The other was of the boys when children, taken with their mother. He had taken both the pictures. He had come across the second one quite recently, and bought a little stand which held it between glass. He used to tell himself it was for his wartime sons and Liz that he had ventured and striven so, to be their hero. So he became, but now he sometimes questioned if he ever really knew Liz. She seldom came into proper focus. He could not reconcile the bright-eyed, coltish young woman – an aspiring journalist herself – whom he joined in such debonair love between assignments in those first years of war, and the un-comprehending loneliness of the mother of his sons, post-war, resentful of his repeated absences, bewildered by his reckless spending. He would come home like an actor between roles to find something expected of him he had no idea how to give. He supposed that (if one was to put it technically) she had fallen in love with the dashing celebrity of the press and he had been captivated by her blind unqualified delight in him.

For a long long time he did not choose to recall things about himself personally – that is, outside his professional achieve-ments – but lately private recollections had come upon him more and more; they would arrive with extraordinary precision at particular moments, involuntarily, especially when he was settling back to sleep in the afternoons. For instance, there was a certain homecoming in those post-war years when he had flown in from Moscow on a Tubolov 103 (though Washington or Paris were a much more usual point of embarkation), landing at Northolt on a grey March afternoon. Steps are wheeled up and the deafening engines die at last. He himself with his felt hat at its customary angle, steps out in his long dark overcoat, slightly flared and with an Astrakhan collar, which he bought in Berlin before the war for forty marks. And galoshes. In one hand his suitcase and in the other his typewriter – this selfsame Olympia, one of the early portables, its handle festooned with the remnants of countless labels acquired on one assignment or another, like notches in an old soldier's rifle-butt. There amid the concourse of meeters and greeters glimpsed through the exit from the customs hall, Liz, straining to catch sight of him, the coltishness flaked by the strain of bringing up the boys all on her own, long weeks at a time, never quite knowing when he would announce his imminent return from one theatre of foreign news or another.

Eager, open-hearted, gregarious Liz – he could attach adjectives to her, but for years now there was no precision to her except when she recurred, in half-sleep or even dreaming, always in the context of those pent homecomings and their blighted hopefulness.

Encumbered by suitcase and typewriter, he pauses to buy a *Star* or *Standard* as they cross to where she has parked the car. MOLOTOV STILL SAYS 'NYET' says the *Star* in big black letters under a strap which reads 'As Big 4 conference breaks up . . .' Only just as they reach the car does she gently tug his typewriter from his hand and his arm is free to slip round her waist.

And then? When she hands him the Hillman keys he can't for a moment remember where the ignition keyhole is.

'Well, how was it, darling?' she asks.

'Moscow always unnerves me.'

Stalin's Moscow, of course.

'Glad to be home again, then?' And she adds, bitter-sweet –
'For a few minutes.'

'They didn't budge one inch on their zone of Germany.
They've got half of Europe for *keeps*. It's not what we thought
we were fighting the war for.'

'Is that the last of the Big Four conferences, then?' she ventures.

'I can't see another.'

'The end of your war at last?'

He knows exactly what she means.

'They want me to do China, my love. Before Mao Tse Tung
wipes Chiang off the map.'

After a little moment she tells him, 'The boys hardly know
you, Gran.'

'Is that what you've persuaded them, my love?'

'They don't need persuading.' He feels he knows the boys
well, but she rubs it in. 'I heard Gavin telling a friend he
wouldn't recognise you in the street if you weren't wearing
your hat.'

'What a dreadfully grown-up thing to say.'

'He was only boasting how important your job was.' She
swallows. 'I can't tell you how hurting it was.' Already she is
nearly crying.

'Who to?'

He shouldn't have said that, because it's a cue.

'For a writer you can be terribly obtuse.'

'I'm not a writer. I'm a reporter.' And mocks himself in a
heavy Russian accent, 'I'm a lackey of the imperialist press
barons.'

This extracts a smile. She tilts her head against his squared
overcoat shoulder. It's a two-hour drive to Essex.

In the boys' bedroom she has decorated the *Morning Post*
wall-map of the world with coloured pins showing where he
has been on assignment. She has made a flag out of a tiny
photograph of his head in his felt hat at the famous angle, cut
from the *Post* in its double-ruled black oval typical of the paper
in those days. The flag is still stuck in at Moscow, and one of
the boys stands on the bed in his pyjamas and moves it to
London. That would be Gavin.

'Why didn't you talk to Mr Stalin, Daddy?'

'He was too busy sending people to Siberia.'

'Didn't you even *see* him?'

'Not this time, Gavin. Though most of the time it felt as if Stalin was with us.'

'Like a ghost, you mean.'

Gavin isn't satisfied, Jones can tell. It's always hard to satisfy Gavin.

'You know when you saw Hitler?'

'That was before the war.'

'Why didn't you shoot him?'

'You can't just go around shooting people.'

'If you shot him there wouldn't have been a war.'

'And you wouldn't have had a daddy.'

'You mean, I wouldn't have even existed.'

Gavin is precocious and likes grown-up words. It was no different then from now.

'Would *I* have existed?' Paul asks. Paul is on Jones's knee, in his pyjamas too.

'If I wouldn't, you wouldn't either,' Gavin states the obvious.

'Why not?' Paul objects, burdening his older brother with his silly questions. But Liz explains.

'They would have shot Daddy before I started you.'

Paul says, 'You started me when Daddy rang up from the airport, didn't you Mummy?'

It was an old Fleet Street joke, among the roving correspondents.

Liz says it was enough talk, it was time the boys were out for the count. And she threatens, *Ten, nine, eight* . . . Paul snuggles against his father and Jones fishes from his pocket two red hammer-and-sickle badges which he begins to safety-pin to the boys' pyjamas, explaining that Mr Molotov gave them to him with best love from Comrade Uncle Joe Stalin.

Gavin is grave again. 'What's Siberia?'

'It's a very cold place, Gavin, full of salt mines and prisoners.'

So Gavin unpins his badge, refusing to take any emblem of evil to bed with him.

And in bed himself that night, much later, after they have made love, Jones half-wakes beside Liz and can just see that she is awake too, with inexplicable tears on her cheeks.

Liz was dead now and the boys forty and thirty-eight. They never visited the island, but just in case they should turn up unexpectedly Jones displayed no portrait of Romy. Though the boys knew well enough it was she that brought him here (everyone knew), no offspring could feel at home with a parent's alternative mate. Even so, he sometimes wondered whether he might not put a picture up without offending the boys. But then, he couldn't be sure that it wasn't because of himself, because he himself couldn't quite bear it, that he had no pictures of Romy up . . . He had enough of them, heaven knows – Romy on the Residency yacht; Romy playing hostess for her father at the Residency; Romy with her father and the Emir and his entourage; Romy, trowel in hand, at her island 'dig'; Romy in a Beirut nightclub on a stolen weekend; Romy asleep on the patio of this very house; Romy looking formally beautiful in a portrait taken by a Bond Street photographer.

The pictures were in drawers and manila envelopes: they had never got around to making an album.

Yet for quite a while after Romy, her things still filled the house – books, prehistoric artefacts, bottles in the bathroom, clothes in wardrobes or drawers. A single hairpin would halt him, make him sit heavily in his chair. The detritus of love is indisposable. He often thought of moving out, in those days; just walking out the door and not coming back, and if it wasn't for the parrot he might have done so.

In the end he had to stay. What else was there for him to do? Who would employ him? By then he had already lived on the island five years; this house seemed to contain all that was left of him; it was Romy who found it for him, she who had pinned up the red and white chequered head-cloth across the window screens when they glassed them over for the newfangled air-conditioners. In the end he tidied up, packed her things away, and kept only her excavated relics on view around him, that was all. During that period of desolation the Emir sent a car for him without warning to fetch him to the palace, but Jones declined to go: he was unshaven at the time and had no serviceable razor-blade. After that the Emir actually called on him and sat with him awhile, bringing a vulgar gift – a consoling tag from the Koran buried in Perspex. He was accompanied by his spoiled young son Hatim.

The Emir asked him what he occupied himself with, and in answer he gestured vaguely towards the pile of typescript pages on his writing-table. This was the book he intended to dedicate to Romy. A London publisher had been enthusiastic about the proposal, talking to him conspiratorially and with too much flattery over lunch at the Savile Club and even paying a small advance. The work was to be a study of mid-century history keyed upon the principal personalities. But he hadn't touched it since Romy.

When at last he turned back to the book, he found the publisher had gone cold. His fame was fading. Television men had become the stars. Nonetheless he did take up the manuscript again and waded on. All these years later it was a massive thing, three hundred thousand words. He could no longer afford a typist to clean-copy his repeated revisions. He alone knew his way through the morass of typescript sheets and freehand notes. There could still be worth in it. He didn't want to die without explaining it to someone.

He thought often about dying, even when his heart was giving no trouble. He seldom missed a siesta unless he was out on an assignment or had a dispatch to file, and thinking about death was like a comforter on the approach to sleep in the afternoon, if no memories happened to flow. He wondered how word of his death might get out. His servant Aziz would report it, of course, and the Emir would hear within a few hours. He hoped he might be granted a little warning and get a call through to McCulloch at the local paper, who perhaps might call London. If the *Post* didn't have an obit ready, it would be best if they didn't get the news late in the day. So McCulloch shouldn't tell them at once if he went later than, say, 3 p.m. London time, simply because whoever they put on to writing the obit wouldn't have time to go through all his cuttings and appreciate the extent of what he'd done: they'd skimp the job. Better for McCulloch to send a 'flash' for the last edition, after the obituary page had been screwed down for the night. The flash might make a couple of inches on page one that night. Then someone could give the whole of the next day to preparing a full-length obit in plenty of time for the first and all subsequent editions . . .

The *Post* was loyal to its former staffers. It was still capable of remembering. It measured its obituaries against genuine professional achievement – irrespective of when. Loyalty to former staffers could still be called a characteristic of Fleet Street, even the trendy, unionised Docklands Fleet Street of today.

2

This particular Friday lunchtime Jones found himself unable to recognise the people with young McCulloch at the Darwish bar. They weren't the self-assured young bankers whose company he favoured.

The mail clerk had handed Jones a cable with his airmailed newspapers and the rest of his correspondence. He settled at one of the window tables and as Abdullah brought him his cold Tuborg and a chilled glass he was opening the cable. It was from the *Post*'s foreign editor and read: 'Suggest 300 maximum on school issue tomorrow for Saturday. Regards Foster.' It must have been sent shortly before Foster left for home the previous evening since it carried a 20.46 GMT slug.

Jones asked, 'Has something been going on at the Asnan school, Abdullah?'

Abdullah's eyes twinkled. 'The Emir has ordered the school to be closed for the present time, Mr Jonas.'

'Oh, has he? Why?'

'He expects the mischief.'

The little fat waiter's eyes always twinkled. Nothing in a bar was serious: alcohol, the infidels' opiate, put everything just out of reach of gravity. Some of the *habitués* had nicknamed him Sunshine.

As Jones was breaking open his third or fourth copy of the *Post*, Sandy McCulloch came across with his little group.

The old man looked up at them with a pained expression.

McCulloch did the introductions. 'This is Lou Rivers of "The World This Week", and Phil and Mick, his camera chappies. All wizards from the telly business.'

They settled round him with the dubious cordiality of people about to touch an acquaintance for a tenner. Rivers said 'Howdy,' and ordered another round of drinks and a second Tuborg for Jones. A shark's tooth bobbed on the fur of his chest among two or three other charms.

Jones enquired indifferently what brought them here, and McCulloch answered for them, '"The World This Week", Gran,' as if that was enough. But Jones stubbornly repeated,

'What brings you here?'

Rivers said, 'You tell me. We've done a couple of bits coming down the Gulf. The Museum of Islamic Art in Kuwait – they gave us a freebie. Yacht club at Dhahran. We've quite a little film in the can on the playgrounds of the Gulf – sheikhs fiddling while Islam burns, the oil price craps out.'

'Playgrounds?'

'Yes. Beach clubs. Gold-plated motors. Crazy palaces. All the decadence.'

'Oh,' Jones said. 'The decadence.' He lit a Kensitas and they saw his hands shake.

'Yes, old son. The decadence, while they slug it out in Meso-potamia. Lousy rich sheikhs. We've some really quite beautiful material, haven't we Phil, really booful? If it makes me sick, with any luck it'll make the viewers sick too.'

'With envy, anyway,' Phil said.

'Not envy at all, Phil. Just sick. I doubt if they'll let us back here in a hurry, that's all.'

'I doubt it, Lou,' Phil agreed.

'Tough stuff,' Jones said, and Rivers followed at once.

'So what's this trouble we hear?'

'Is there trouble?' Jones asked, as vague as could be.

'You should know, Gran,' McCulloch answered. 'You always know.'

'I know nothing. I've only just been told the Emir's shut the school. London tells me.' He flapped his cable.

'You said this bloke knew everything, Sandy,' Rivers commented across him.

Jones regarded Rivers sadly. 'I get all my information from people like you.'

Rivers said, 'That's what we journalists are for, I suppose.'

'I'm a journalist,' Jones told him.

'Eh?'

'The *Morning Post*. Granville Jones, *Morning Post*,' he

16

repeated with a courtly distance and watched the blank puzzlement in Rivers' eyes. He picked up a copy of the airmailed *Post*.

'Right. Great,' Rivers said. 'What the hell are we doing? London can't have wanted us to come down here for a closed school.'

'Shit-awful television,' Phil the cameraman confirmed. 'A closed school.'

'Reuters are sending,' McCulloch assured him. 'Shaun Carew's coming down from Kuwait this afternoon. They smell trouble at the oilfield.'

'A strike?' Rivers asked.

'There isn't a union. Not officially,' McCulloch said.

'Who's this bloke Al Baker, Gran?' Rivers asked. 'Let's have some detail: who's this bloke Al Baker?'

Jones looked up slowly from the *Post*.

'Who's Al Baker?' Rivers persisted.

'Who?' Jones blinked rheumily.

'Al Baker, the labour leader. Where does he come from?'

Jones addressed himself to McCulloch. 'What does he mean, "Where does he come from?"'

Rivers interrupted, 'I mean, *Where does he come from?*'

'Fuad Al-Bakr comes from here. Where else?'

'My people say I ought to get an interview with him.'

'You can't. If he's on the island at all, he's in hiding.'

'Well, where does he hide? That's what I'm asking.'

'Oh are you?'

'We'd pay,' Rivers said. 'Have another, old son. Tuborg? Waiter! I say, what is it? Four Heinekens, one Tuborg. More nuts . . . Beg pardon if I was a bit sharp, old son. I've been on the hop too long. All these late nights in the playgrounds earning my living.' He patted Jones on the knee, rattling a bracelet with his name on it, which was perhaps meant to imply to women in cocktail bars or alongside swimming-pools that his job exposed him to real battles in a real war and only by the bracelet would his news-martyred body be identified.

What kind of boys were these, Jones thought, playing at danger? And simultaneously Rivers was saying, 'What kind of a bloke is he, then? This Al Baker, wotsit. I mean, you must have known him man and boy.'

'What you would expect,' Jones replied indistinctly, raising his newspaper, cutting them off. He hadn't the least intention of telling this Rivers or even McCulloch that he had never actually met Al-Bakr. He'd as good as done so twenty-five years ago; and the fact that a meeting hadn't actually taken place didn't make a scrap of difference to his understanding of Al-Bakr . . . To be precise, it was the third day after his arrival on the island on his first visit. The previous day he had met Romy.

'What might that mean,' Rivers said, '– "What you would expect?"'

Jones kept his paper up. His sight had blurred, and he was in the old fish market, twenty-five years before, climbing out of Romy's Land-rover.

'What Gran means is,' McCulloch was saying, 'Al-Bakr's the typical old guard republican leftist who's longing for real power after – what, Gran? – twenty-five years in exile? He sees the Gulf Liberation Movement like the PLO. Years ago the Emir persuaded us to put him on St Helena for a couple of years. Right, Gran?'

'So I recall,' Jones said from behind his newspaper, but he was with Romy in the fish market. She is in her bush shirt and trousers and floppy porridge-bowl hat. All the Arab marketmen know her. She is expounding to him: they were the oldest race of traders in the world. Six thousand years ago the ancestors of these stall-holders were in business right here – or just down the coast at her site. 'Copper, tin, salt, limes, juniper,' she reels off. 'Frankincense, sesame oil, flax, pearls.' 'Girls?' Jones queries, and she shoots him a glance of quizzical reprimand, for nothing is admitted between them yet.

'Slaves, anyway,' she says. 'Now, look and learn. This is a *binte nakhoda*.' Blue and yellow. 'These crayfish they call *rubiyan*.'

She has spotted him sneaking a look at his watch and clouds instantly. And he is protesting it was his job, his profession. '*Your* profession is excavating sunken prehistoric ports. *My* job is interviewing popular firebrands.'

'You want to betray my father's trust,' she retorts icily.

'If I see Al-Bakr,' he begins, and her head gives a tiny tight shake at him for mentioning the forbidden firebrand's name in the hearing of the marketmen. He proceeds more quietly, 'If I see ahem, I wouldn't file anything without talking to the Emir too. Your father says he's perfectly articulate.'

'The Emir would never stand for it. Thingumme's about to be deported. The Emir wants him forgotten.'

'I could give the Emir the main crack of the whip – lead with an interview with him. But I'd need a quote from Thingumme too.'

'He'd never consent – *his* views being balanced by Thingumme. A complete upstart. An excitable student managed by the Russians. He spent three years in Odessa, you know.'

'Hero of the oil workers even so,' Jones insists. 'The Emir's income depends entirely on oil. It's what the story's about.'

She looks up hot and perturbed under the rim of her floppy hat. 'The Emir won't even know you're on the island. It's against all the rules.'

'Your father's told him.'

'The Wazir told him?'

'So he said. Look, Romy, house arrest doesn't necessarily mean incommunicado.'

He can read the injury in her face. 'If you press ahead with it, it'll spoil . . .' she begins, but doesn't finish.

They occupy different worlds. When she drops him off at the hotel – the original Darwish – these is a cable waiting for him from his Foreign Editor. SUGGEST 850 WORDER MAXIMUM GULF ROUNDUP INSIDE PROFRIDAY CUMBAKER EMIR CONTEST HOOK STOP HAST PIC BAKER QUERY CANST UPMOP BEIRUT HOMEWARDING STOP INFORMING LIZ ACCORDINGLY REGARDS BILL.

Jones asks his taxi-driver to take him to wherever Al-Bakr is being held. The man pretends not to understand, then not to know. Jones makes a thin roll of a couple of dirty banknotes and pokes it over the driver's shoulder from the back seat like a doctor's implement going into an orifice. They set off and the driver pulls up several yards short of a carefully inconspicuous bungalow on the edge of the town. Jones steps out with his

Rolleiflex round his neck. He can hear all the muezzins, one after another, launching into the call to midday prayer. No one appears to be guarding the bungalow, but as he approaches he can see through an open doorway a policeman in uniform playing backgammon with a weedy young man in civilian shirt and trousers, and another uniformed man to one side drinking tea from a glass. When the weedy young man catches sight of Jones he guesses immediately and reaches for his black and white chequered head-cloth to look his part. He is not more than twenty-five and already balding – a scrap of a man with delicate nervous fingers and his spectacles held together by tape. The policemen have looked up puzzled: they are expecting no English official.

By the time they have moved to the threshold, fitting on their caps, they are surprised to see the tall figure sauntering back towards the taxi.

That was as near as Jones ever got to Al-Bakr. A quarter of a century ago. It was the first time in his life that he had allowed another consideration to take precedence over the assignment.

Rivers had apparently asked, 'Why shut the school?' and McCulloch was explaining that the old Emir knew that Al-Bakr, from hiding, was recruiting rank-and-file Arab oil and port workers into an underground union and presumably feared the infection might spread to the big secondary school where bored, pretentious students, some of them twenty years of age or more, were attempting to secure qualifications a changing world seemed to expect. Everyone knew they were undisciplined and indulged by their parents.

A voice intervened from behind the raised copy of the *Post*. 'There's no groundswell of opposition.'

'That so?' Rivers had to say.

'If you think you've come for a big story,' Jones added, 'settle down for a long wait. Months. Years, probably.'

'We don't think we've come for anything, do we, Phil, do we, Mick? It's London trying to be clever.'

When the old man brought his paper down at last it was like

a curtain rising on a dead past. First he regarded Rivers, then McCulloch. 'Are you leading on this school?' he said.

'It wouldn't be very tactful,' McCulloch answered. 'We'll run a single column down the right-hand side. We'll lead on the loan to Egypt.'

'What are *we* meant to do?' Rivers protested. Events conspired to frustrate Rivers, which, for someone of his stature, they had little right to do. 'We might as well get some lunch and take a swim, eh fellows? They give us lunch by the pool in this place?' He fingered his shark's tooth. 'So you can't get us an interview with this Al Whatsit, Gran? What about the imprisoned Prince, the Man in the Iron Mask?'

'Hatim?'

'Yes, Hatim. Love 'im, Hatim.'

'He's under house arrest. In a villa.'

'Couldn't we visit?'

'Not possibly.'

'Just shoot the villa? The comings and goings.'

Phil affirmed, 'It's shit-awful television.'

'I doubt if you'll get a picture of the villa,' Jones said.

'I bet we bloody can. We've got to shoot *something*.'

'You'd get yourselves arrested,' Jones told him.

'For taking a picture of the outside of a villa? What sort of a fascist is this Emir? Why don't we see the old codger himself? That's what we've got to do.'

'He doesn't give interviews.'

'He'll bloody well give interviews when the people have dumped him in the dock.'

'The people like him,' Jones corrected.

'Do they, Sandy?' Rivers asked.

Jones picked up the *Post* again.

'By and large,' McCulloch endorsed.

'So when did he hold an election? No, look – we've got to go and do him.'

Jones wasn't going to tell him again that the Emir didn't give interviews. Let him find out.

Others began to swell the group – a London merchant banker, flabby and amiable and sharp, with whom McCulloch let it be thought he had a private understanding; young Carew from Reuters, a weasel of a man, who it emerged had made a good half dozen telephone calls within an hour of flying in; the oil company's chief public affairs man, a wry American, with his cards, which perhaps were not high, held very close to his chest. All were by way of pecking fragments off of one another: when it came to the crunch, these Arabs weren't predictable, they occupied their own, strange, Mussulman world . . . They treated Jones respectfully enough and sometimes consulted him on a point of fact, but as the conversation found its feet they paid him less and less heed. The consensus was that something was brewing. Fuad Al-Bakr, everyone seemed to know, had been smuggled back into the island in the past few days. The oil town was thick with rumour.

More beer came: Jones was damned if he was going to have a round put down to his bar account: he hadn't asked them to join him in the first place.

The talk became such a mush of blather that he could only distinguish the recurring misjudgments like grit in gruel. Life seemed to him interminably long and mankind did not improve. He wondered what it was that was supposed to make mankind so important.

He pushed himself up and went to the telephone booth in the foyer. He felt wobbly and it took him two minutes to remember the private number of the Diwan, the Emir's principal secretary. Nobody answered. What did they suppose, these half-fledged know-alls? That the old Emir craved power? Hoarded it like a miser – he who had been born to it? It was an antique habit, an obscure and burdensome obligation. Like remaining alive. He dialled the palace number. An assistant secretary said the Diwan was in a meeting. Jones left a message that he had called. When he returned to the bar-room he sat by himself. He drafted his brief dispatch with another Tuborg. The school was closed, he wrote, as a precaution against agitation among groups of elderly students, known to be bored and restless, by elements of the so-called Gulf Liberation Movement directed by Fuad Al-Bakr, whose recent pronouncements, released outside the island, had become increasingly inflammatory. He copied it out in capital letters on a sheet of hotel writing-paper and gave it to the head porter to send down to Cable and Wireless.

Then he ate hot meat pie and green beans which Abdullah brought him from the bar, and drank two brandies because he was not feeling himself. The group he had left were still yattering away, occasionlly breaking into laughter – the hooting of Rivers, the television anchorman (as he understood they were called), being louder than the rest. He considered a noticeable laugh to indicate a flaw in personality. They gave him no further attention, and when the porter came with the receipt from Cable and Wireless he realised they were all gone.

3

It was well after 4 p.m. as he emerged into the sun, climbed into his old Packard and drove noisily home. He was a little drunk and profoundly depressed. How dare these young puppies from London insult him to his face? As for the Reuters pipsqueak, sitting there drinking little and giving nothing away, he hadn't consulted him on anything. He, Jones, happened not to know for certain whether Al-Bakr was back on the island and he was damned if he was going to find out unless he was obliged to.

What was the GLM, in any case? These credulous young reporters talked of it as if it were a genuine political force! It was nothing but a handful of recalcitrants and ex-students, motivated by envy, who had picked up a notion of fading socialist populism in the West. By putting out a few press releases they earned themselves wads of money from Libya and elsewhere which in turn enabled them to open offices in certain capitals. If the Western media didn't take their pretensions at face value, they'd be seen as the semi-educated talking-shop they were. If he, Jones, let off one little bomb in a United States Information Service reading room and got Abdullah the waiter to call a press conference in Tripoli in the name of, let's say, the 'Pan-Arab Revolutionary Council', these same simpletons would turn up with their notebooks and television cameras and scatter the world with forecasts of proletarian upheaval wherever a king or emir still ruled.

As he entered the dark passageway beyond his front door, he heard the telephone ringing in the bedroom. He wasn't going to run for it and, by the time he reached it, the ringing had stopped. If it's London, he thought, they'll put the call in again: it wasn't yet 2 p.m. in London. He kicked off his sandals and lay on the bed against his pillows. He loosened his trousers and thought how immensely ancient his feet looked. Ancient and mute and wise. Had all his old wisdom gone to his feet? He felt an obscure loyalty to those gnarled, chipped extremities that had tramped the world with him, slaved for him, expected nothing in return. He realised he was drunk. He often noticed how drink would unpin his body and make it a random aggregate of parts and features which he himself looked upon from somewhere else.

He did not wake until 8 p.m. Darkness surrounded him. He sat up. His whole body felt as if a weight had settled on it. He slid his old feet into his flip-flops and shuffled through to the bathroom and then into the kitchen. He tipped out cornflakes and poured on evaporated milk. Only a drop in the tin. He looked around vainly for another. Ants were moving over the sugar like columns of redcoats in the snow. He couldn't bear cornflakes with too little milk. He opened a can of beer and took it back to the bedroom. He undressed now, and got into bed. He drank the beer slowly, and fell asleep again. At about 3 a.m. he woke. He lay awake in the dark, thinking. He had slept now almost continuously for about ten hours. He couldn't sleep any more.

About an hour later he got up and pottered through to the *majlis*. It was a stifling night. He switched on the air-conditioning and it shuddered into life with a terrible effort. Still in his sarong, he sat down at the table laden with the disordered typescripts of his book. He took a plain sheet of foolscap and fitted it into his old portable. In the top right-hand corner he typed the Post Box number of the Darwish and the date. Of his sons, he chose Paul to write to because Gavin was intolerant of him and always had been. He could tell that was still so from the tone of Gavin's occasional letters, and particularly from the letters of Gavin's wife (another scientist: Gavin had met her at university) when he wrote enquiring about the grandchildren: neither she nor Gavin ever asked anything about his life – never a query, never a speculation. Their rare letters fulfilled a dry duty.

The dedication to Romy was still there in the typescript: he sat for a long time questioning himself if it was necessary to change it or drop it, for the boys' sake. He crossed it out and restored it by hand two or three times, before finally deciding.

He said to himself that Gavin would take exception either way, since he had chosen to look upon the very profession of a roving reporter as incompatible with marriage and parenthood. Paul would bear with it. Paul knew about him in a way Gavin never would.

He did not draft the letter first, but went at it straight out, x-ing over when he mis-keyed or started into a sentence that looked like working out unsatisfactorily.

'My dear Paul,' he typed, 'I want you to take over my book *The Men that Made History* should I die before the project is complete.

'I know that you are very busy and that you may find this rather a tall order. But I hope I can persuade you it will be worth your while.

'You may wish to seek the co-operation of a young modern historian from a neighbouring university. If you do, I ask you not to pass the real responsiblity to him. If you give a free hand to anyone else I am afraid he will simply lift the material and produce a book of his own. The book is mine and there is quite a lot of good material in it.

'It is not far from being finished, although I have not yet decided on a cut-off date. The main requirement is to dovetail in the interpolations and notes, some of which as you see are in my handwriting and therefore difficult for most people.'

He paused here and shuffled all the way back to his bedroom to fetch his cigarettes. The night was quiet and heavy with heat. He could hear the crickets in his garden and Suleiman's tree-frogs from across the wall. That was all. He noticed his parrot was awake and he thought, why shouldn't it be – I am. He took his Kensitas back to the *majlis*, and lit one up. It helped him proceed.

'I am only writing this letter because lately I have grown very tired. I have been experiencing what old Winston called "the sullen advance of decrepitude". If I had the money for a proper secretary the book would soon be finished.

'Let me assure you, my dear boy, that if you spend a little

money on having it pulled together, you will get it all back, and more too, when it is published. Some of it is sensational. Future historians of the period can hardly afford to overlook it.

'Don't dismiss this as the ravings of an old man.' (He first typed 'lonely old man', but he didn't want Paul to think of him as pathetic.) 'My opportunities to witness the major events of our century were unique. It is not relevant that I am forgotten now.'

He kept his cigarette in his mouth all through, with the butt going soggy and the ash dropping on his sarong; and as he typed the telephone began to ring in his bedroom. It rang unheard for fully two minutes. Then it stopped, and almost immediately began again. It continued for a further half minute and stopped again. It was about 4.25 a.m. local time.

He had a feeling there was something else he ought to say to Paul, but he couldn't summon whatever it might be. He rather fancied it might be something to do with the dedication, but that was surely much too big a subject to open up here. If he left the dedication in, Paul would surely respect that. Now he wondered how to conclude the letter. This wasn't the place for pleasantries about the family. So he just typed 'Love from'. Then he looked back at the date. Should it carry today's date? He wasn't intending to send if off today, so perhaps he should leave it undated. He didn't know when he might send it: he just wanted to have the letter ready written, in case. He turned back the roller and typed brackets round the date. Then he pulled the sheet off the typewriter, read it through carefully, touching it up in ink here and there, making little scoops under the x-ings out to link one word with the next, as he had been taught to do half a century ago for the sub-editors. He signed 'Daddy' at the foot of the page, typed the envelope and propped it against an amphora where anyone would notice it.

He began to put in order the draft sections he had already rough-typed, then the pages of notes he had made; but after a while he was side-tracked by a missing source and became engrossed in a book about the Vatican between 1940 and 1942 when hedging its bets against an ultimate Nazi defeat. Because

27

it was Saturday and there was no Sunday edition of the *Post* to file for, he did not trouble to tune into the BBC World Service news at 7 a.m.

Had he done so he would have heard the lead item reporting, in full, a broadcast from the island monitored in the previous hour.

'The broadcast,' said the BBC, 'announced the replacement of the ruler of the Gulf island emirate of Hawar by his younger son. The seven-minute announcement, according to the broadcast, was given by Hatim bin Ahmed al-Asnan, who has been held in detention by order of his father, the Emir Ahmed, for the past eighteen months.

'The broadcast stated that the Emir had signed a decree appointing his son, Hatim, as Regent, on the grounds of his age and failing health, and that Hatim had assumed the role of President-Regent. The country would be ruled henceforth as a republic, and, as President-Regent, Hatim bin Ahmed had already appointed Fuad Al-Bakr, leader of the hitherto banned Gulf Liberation Movement, as Prime Minister.

'All international treaties were to be honoured, the broadcast stated, but the agreement with the American-controlled oil company, which operates the island's oil production on behalf of the State's Ministry of Petroleum Production, was under review. Immediate recognition had been accorded by the Soviet Union, which, the broadcast claimed, had already promised defence and technical assistance.

'Any person making a disturbance or carrying a weapon would be shot on sight. A curfew would be strictly in force between sunset and dawn until further notice.

'The broadcast ended with an exhortation to the people to remain calm and loyal to the Government and the country, which had entered upon what it called a new and glorious phase of its history.

'Our Diplomatic Correspondent says the Emir Ahmed has ruled Hawar firmly and without significant opposition for thirty-two years. He saw his relatively small island territory emerge from poverty and obscurity to become one of the richest states in the world, in terms of per capita income and reserves of wealth. Its known oil and gas reserves, onshore and offshore, rank third in the Middle East.'

The BBC's broadcast was followed by a brief comment from the Diplomatic Correspondent to the effect that if an abrupt change of political direction had indeed taken place in the island, the economic, political, and strategic consequences for the Free World could be profound.

Jones, sorting through the massive typescript in the *majlis*, heard none of this.

When his servant failed to make his customary appearance at 9 a.m., he was not surprised. Aziz was sickly and often too sorry for himself to fulfil his tasks. In any case, Jones had no wish to be disturbed. He boiled himself a cup of coffee and worked all through the morning getting into the correct page order the many interpolations he had made to his original draft. It was still something of a mess – the gaps unexplained, the parallel versions likewise. But it had a rough coherence now, and when he had decided he had done enough he was profoundly relieved, for his health was not good today. It seemed that every movement he made was ill-judged as if he had wrenched his whole body unawares.

It was already midday before he flip-flopped through to his outer door to bring in the local English-language daily. It was not there. Normally it would be lying on his doorstep. He looked up and down the empty alley. He supposed it had been pilfered by a passer-by. At about 1 p.m. he picked up the telephone in the bedroom to ask the head porter at the Darwish if he had a play-back wire from London. His line was dead.

He wondered vaguely if this was his own world gently closing in on him. No paper, no telephone, no servant. He was out of tinned milk, and the shop would be shut now in the heat of the day. He had cornflakes, sugar, tea and coffee. He had half a piece of flat Arab bread. He ate the bread very slowly in the malodorous kitchen, and drank a beer out of the can. He took a handful of seed and opened the door of the parrot's cage. He took the parrot into the bedroom and began to feed it seed, eating every alternate seed himself. On his bed once more he picked up the book about the Vatican in wartime but he couldn't concentrate and began to wonder who could have foretold then that some forty years on he would be here all alone and almost entirely forgotten on this remote sand-dune of an island whose highest natural elevation was a hundred and eighty feet (he who grew up in the Shropshire hills!) He can recall with precision talking in El Vino's in Fleet Street with the Foreign Editor about the delight of the PM (Macmillan, of course) with his 'wind of change', stealing the Opposition's clothes, and of another sell-out in the offing. 'Those Gulf sheikhs could go down like ninepins if we clear out,' the Foreign Editor comments. 'Mind you, I know nothing.'

Jones is about to set off for Assam to cover the Naga rebellion – he, a smoker, a steady drinker, already well into middle age, tramping through the Indian jungle. They speculate together if he would be up to it. The Gulf has cropped up as a mere afterthought. Should he just drop in on the island on the way home? the Foreign Editor suggests. The island holds the key to the area. 'You can bring back a yashmak for Liz – or a string of pearls. I believe they still dive for them there. Right, Gran?' A suggestion, merely. Jones could have brushed it aside. It was the first of the strokes of caprice, that he later came to pinpoint, on which his destiny was to hinge. Hence the precision of his memory.

There is no hurry for the Naga rebellion, and the discussion turns on which day Jones should leave for Calcutta, the jumping-off point. The Nagas would still be revolting whether he caught a flight on the Wednesday or Thursday, and on Wednesday Paul was going back to school for his last term.

'Then what?' the Foreign Editor enquires.

'Oh – university. Less expensive, thank God. He gets a grant.'

'He'll join Gavin, I suppose.'

'At Sussex? It's become instantly fashionable. I'm not sure that I trust that – it can become just as instantly unfashionable.'

'Where's Gavin aiming when he comes down? Follow in father's footsteps?'

'Gavin's a science man,' Jones explains. 'He treats newspapers as a sort of disease.'

'And you carry the disease, Gran?'

'You have it exactly.'

'What are the symptoms?'

'Absences from hearth and home.' Jones is gazing into his dry martini. 'It stems from what he sees as loyalty to his mamma. When I told him not so long ago that I loved her he said he "disagreed". I asked what he meant. He said if I loved her I would have given her a divorce.'

'Has she asked for a divorce, Gran?'

'Certainly not. But she does like to say, "What's the point of being married?"'

'She got someone else?'

'Sometimes I rather wish she had.'

The Foreign Editor is a heavy kindly man. He likes to pretend a wide ignorance about people and the world. That way he finds out about everything.

Jones looks up at the assembly of newspapermen: there's no other life he knows. The Foreign Editor waits for him.

'When the boys were young she used to have a map of the world on their bedroom wall and wherever I was she'd stick a flag in – she'd made a flag with my head on it. Nowadays, once I'm out of the home, I don't think I get a mention. It's a sort of policy: make enough of a vacuum and I could be sucked back in.' He adds, 'Gavin's been quite an active vacuum.'

'You ever want to chuck it in?'

'How could I, Bill? What else am I good for? I've got the mark of Cain.' And when the Foreign Editor speculates unconvincingly, that there would always be a desk job for him, Jones can only return a contemptuous silence.

'What about the younger boy?'

Paul's different. 'If Paul's offered love, he doesn't look it in the mouth. They ticked him off at school for keeping my letters in his collar box.'

The Foreign Editor sympathises. To get it exactly right is a known impossibility. 'For most wives it's the sheer predictability that stifles them. They want to do a Madame Bovary.'

'Liz does the Citizen's Advice Bureau twice a week,' Jones says. And the garden of course. Every spring and summer he has to learn the names of the flowers anew.

He couldn't recall taking Paul back to boarding-school that last term. But he remembered joining the Naga rebels and the brutality of the Indian army which contrasted so unhappily with Nehru's lofty international moralising. The Indians' pique at Jones's reports infected the British consul in Calcutta who declined to endorse his passport for the stop he meant to make on the way home – the island Emirate in the Persian Gulf. He could still hear the consul's papery voice, trying to be facetious. 'We have a *Protective* Treaty with those Arabs.' He looks up at Jones. 'There's a spot of unrest there, I need hardly say. The ruler wouldn't appreciate our flooding the island with newspaper reporters.'

'I'm not exactly a flood.'

'You never know who else.' The consul is a dandy and at the acme of his powers.

'I just thought I'd overnight there on my way to London.'

'You mean, your paper's not actually asked you to go there?'

'Actually it has.'

'Would you happen to have any evidence of that?'

'Will it make any difference?'

'That depends.'

Jones fishes out a cable and passes it over reluctantly. It reads, HMG HAS AGREED DEPORT UNION LEADER AL BAKER SAINT HELENAWARDS STOP WANT YOU SOONEST GULF PROINTERVIEW BAKER AND ISLAND EMIR REGARDS BILL.

'Who is Bill?' the consul smirks.

'Foreign Editor.'

'He seems to think Al-Bakr is an Englishman.'

'An understandable slip.'

The consul turns back to the passport.

'You know you're described here as "Traveller and Writer?"'

'I was aware.'

'Is that quite fair?'

'To whom?'

'To whom it may concern.'

'You mean, to nasty little regimes under our protection that want to keep the press out, so that the world needn't know whose balls they are twisting off at police headquarters.'

For this he gets another pearly smirk. 'I'm bound to tell you, Mr Jones, that by joining those Naga rebels you haven't done yourself any good in India. Or indeed, us.'

It isn't difficult to construct a flight home via the Persian Gulf so that a stopover on the island is inevitable. The solitary immigration officer on duty at the island's primitive airport requires him to sleep on a wooden bench right there in the arrivals area. Jones concurs with a puzzled grace. But would the official kindly arrange for somebody to collect the draft of money awaiting him at the British bank in town? (Jones has already perceived that there are no facilities for eating, or even a lavatory, in this arrivals area. There's no trick he doesn't know.) In due course another official of superior authority is summoned to consider Jones's disingenuous request, and since authority is worthless unless exercised, the junior official is overruled. With a bouncing motion between inky pad and page – a little movement fixed in Jones's mind for the rest of his life as the second capricious twist of the combination that was to unlock his private destiny – a 24-hour visa is stamped in his 'unfair' passport.

A scarred taxi carries him to a venerable hotel, the Darwish, built long ago for some other purpose on a spit of land, and here a perspiring Greek provides him with a peeling room far too high-ceilinged and spacious for the grinding, weeping air-conditioner to render cool. So Jones puts an end to the machine's vain struggle, and opens the french windows upon an opal sea, a harbour arm, and, there beyond, a hunched dun-coloured Arab town of roofs that were also evening rooms, and tight alleys, hidden garden sanctuaries, and minarets.

The British Resident is known, so it seems, by the Arab honorific for trusted advisers as 'the Wazir'. Alternatively he is Sir Geoffrey Burton. He has taken pains over the years to keep the island free of the international press, but once Granville Jones of the *Post* has slipped in he is wise enough not only not to have him thrown out, but to have him in for a chat. Jones finds himself being received with a wily humour, about which he can do little, since *he* knows that *Burton* knows he stole into the island, and has done so because young Al-Bakr has pushed the place into the news. Burton, like the consul at Calcutta, reminds Jones that the island is not a British colony, as such. It is rather, he says – and at this point all comparison with the consul ends – 'a colony of the sun and sea and Allah. They are the arbiters. We provide a little shade, a little spring of worldly wisdom.'

From the upper floor of the Residency, desert and sea lie beyond the verandah in three directions, and a brand new sparkling palace. And, much closer, the Union Jack atop its mast in the compound. By clutching this mast, slaves win freedom by the hand of Britain's Resident, as ancient treaty has decreed. Burton has come round from behind the desk and has settled beside Jones in an easy chair. On the wall hang two matching photographic portraits, one of the Queen of England and one of the Emir of this island who, in his head-cloth, has the aspect of a buzzard. Soon enough the conversation veers away from the affairs of the island, with Burton doing most of the talking, to the affairs of the world where Jones's views are sought. Gone already is the wily humour. Jones draws back the thread of talk so that it weaves between them freely, in and out of the region. A great slow fan in the ceiling accompanies their *tour d'horizon*, for the new-fangled air-conditioner has yet to penetrate the British Residency. Jones supposes Burton seldom has anyone to talk to with much to add to his own 'spring of worldly wisdom'. Within the past twelve months Jones himself has talked with Nasser in Cairo, Khrushchev in the Kremlin, and the Shah in Iran.

Both men are of an age, though Burton senior by ten years or so; both are brown from the sun, both in their way powerful men, vigorous, though Jones is lean and tall and the other chunky. They are curiously complementary in bearing and in mind, the one rooted deep in a single theatre, Arabia and its

Gulf, the other commanding an extraordinary global eclecticism. Jones's eyes drift to the distance and he reflects on this harsh flat treeless waste growing to be such a crucible of politics and human rivalry. When his time is up, it comes to him as no surprise to find himself invited to dinner that very evening (it will mean at least a 36-hour extension to his visa): their discussion has a good way to run yet.

Burton is at once on to the veranda, calling to someone in the compound beneath.

'Will you tell Purvis, my dear, there'll be one extra tonight.'

'What's that, Wazir?'

The woman below, Jones can see, is in a bush shirt and trousers and an army issue denim hat.

'One extra for dinner tonight.'

'Right-o.'

It occurs to Jones that Wazir Burton may have married a second time to have a wife so apparently young.

The two other guests that evening are already there in dinner jackets when Purvis, the ducal Goan butler as black as your hat, admits Jones in a crumpled suit. Their hostess, *soignée* now and deeply bronzed in a white cocktail dress wrapped in a V across her bosom, her heavy sunbleached hair pinned up in a chignon, comes forward instantly to put Jones at his ease. She is scarcely past thirty, yet every inch the experienced diplomatic hostess.

'You are Mr Granville Jones. I'm so glad you could join us. I'm Romy Burton.'

Jones affects to feeling lanky and unkempt. 'I fear I've come without the appropriate wedding garment. I hope it won't mean wailing and gnashing of teeth.'

'It doesn't matter in the least, Mr Jones. Do I say a "jot or tittle"? But' – eyeing his mock-awkward stance – 'if it'll put you at your ease, I'll fetch you one of the Wazir's bow-ties.'

Jones says, 'I'm probably best as my scruffy self. It's a sign of a defunct newspaperman when he starts aping the gentry.'

'Come and meet Mr Stuart-Smith who's just been building a most glorious new palace for the Emir.'

Stuart-Smith exudes a tennis-court fitness and has a hand-shake like a forehand drive.

'And this is a very old friend of ours, Richard Fenton, from our consulate-general in Jeddah. Richard is honouring us by spending a few days of his leave with us.'

Fenton isn't old at all, not yet thirty-five, but one of those whose brain has sucked up his bodily vigour as if through a long straw. 'We were just talking of you, Mr Jones. I see you've been "writing up" the Naga rebels in Assam.' He pronounces 'writing up' like a term of daring. 'It must have been dreadfully strenuous.'

Stuart-Smith gives a condescending smile. 'You chaps do get around.'

'What brings you *here*?' Romy asks, but Fenton intervenes archly,

'Not the island "rebels", I trust.'

'My paper asked me to mop up the situation on the way home.'

'Ah, the instant expert,' says Stuart-Smith. 'With his mop,' adds Fenton, the instant wit. And both dart Romy Burton glances of complicity, though neither, it seems, achieves a response. Fenton has long wrists and a prominent Adam's apple.

Burton himself now enters in a white dinner-jacket and Romy signs to Purvis to put the cold cucumber soup on the table.

'Wazir,' she says, 'Mr Jones was just about to tell us why he's here.' But deflects her own challenge at once. 'You're the first pukka journalist from Fleet Street I think we've ever invited in.'

'I wasn't really invited,' Jones demurs. 'I slipped by.'

To which Burton adds, 'Having done so, I thought we ought to make the most of him.'

'I'm a lucky butterfly,' Jones says, 'with a day to live and do my mopping up.'

'It's possible that the Emir might be interested to hear from you what Nasser had to say about the Gulf.'

Stuart-Smith is not to be outdone and assures Jones, on behalf of them all, 'The Emir's a very good chap, you'll find.' He had, after all, awarded Mr Stuart-Smith and his company a lucrative contract.

Romy, at one end of the dining-table, has Jones on her right. The relatively larger gap between her age – hardly less than thirty years – and Burton's seems to Jones to diminish the twenty-year gap between hers and *his*. Her vitality affects him in a strange way, as if his body were a parched landscape webbed with dried-up irrigation channels that her river flooded. The whole region could become virid and beautiful and the river itself discover its forgotten purpose. (Years later, he became uncertain if he thought of the river at the dinner party or dreamt it that night.)

During the dessert the overweening Stuart-Smith appends to a tedious item of pretended confidence he has let slip, 'Of course, I must be careful what I say,' with a facetious half-glance at Jones.

'I don't think you need worry about Mr Jones's discretion,' Burton assures him from his end of the table.

But Stuart-Smith is in waggish spirits. 'What was it Churchill said about the "privilege of the whore" – if our charming hostess will forgive the quotation?'

Jones reminds him that Churchill was a journalist himself. Could Mr Stuart-Smith be referring to Baldwin who spoke of the press having 'power without responsibility – the role of the harlot throughout the ages'?

'That's exactly it,' Stuart-Smith exclaims, oblivious, in his self-delight, of who it is that has provided what he chooses to take as an endorsement.

'You needn't ever be afraid,' Burton assures him, 'of finding harlots at my table.'

Jones comments, 'I never quite understood Baldwin. I would match the press's sense of responsibility against the politicians' any day.'

'Oh – steady on,' Fenton protests.

Stuart-Smith scents more support. 'You writer-chappies are after headlines, Mr Jones. Anything goes. Not with you personally, of course.'

It is the disclaimer that riles.

'I don't know what newspaper Mr Stuart-Smith reads. *Reveille* perhaps?' Jones turns from one to the other. 'In the Korean war, in a couple of years, no less than seven British journalists were killed, all colleagues of mine, mostly friends too. Seven of about twenty, in all. Mr Stuart-Smith would say they were after the headlines. I would prefer to say they were after the facts.'

Stuart-Smith argues with the finesse of a charging rhino. 'With great respect,' he returns nastily, 'I've seldom known a journalist get his facts right. Not in my line of business.'

Jones enquires whether he would be right in thinking he liked to keep the press out of his line of business?

'Most certainly.'

'Except when you need them,' Jones says. 'Then you feed them.'

Stuart-Smith gives a thick cynical smile, from the inviolability of a fat contract. But Jones taunts him now.

'Lenin and Stalin shared your view of the press. For the truth, try *Pravda*.'

'Oh, fisticuffs!' exclaims Fenton.

Burton intervenes. 'You wouldn't allow, Jones, by and large, that the press leans to the sensational?'

'The press leans, Sir Geoffrey, towards what people in various readership brackets will read. At least, that is so in a free country. People are interested in what is unexpected and new. Hence the term "news".'

'Just what I mean.' Stuart-Smith has turned for a second charge. 'You chaps twist it to get headlines.' He throws Romy a self-congratulatory look.

But she has dug him a little pit, taking her time.

'Don't you think, Mr Stuart-Smith, it is often a mistake to generalise.'

She makes this much more of a statement of truth than a question, and the precision of her tone somehow has Stuart-Smith with his horn in the earth and all four legs in the air, so much so that her quick triumphant glance to Jones contains pity for the man.

'Well, Jones,' Burton says, 'you have secured my daughter's support.'

It is the first time since childhood that Jones can remember his face turning hot from confusion. Burton's *daughter*. But of course. Burton a *widower*, naturally.

'That was indeed unexpected,' he murmurs, rattled by his obtuseness, though quite why so rattled, his error not having been betrayed, he could not tell. The reason is of course that it is already too late to put in place the proper divide between his generation and this woman's. And soon afterwards he could see this idiotic misapprehension to have been the third stroke of caprice, like the last digit of a combination lock, that opened him to . . .

4

. . . to love.

When Jones woke again it was already four in the afternoon. The parrot had left its droppings on the floor and the chair. He propped himself up and tuned to the BBC World Service and was a minute late for the news. The first item was almost identical to the 7 a.m. broadcast that he had missed. The only additional piece of information was of a complete news blackout from the island: all telecommunications had been severed and the airport was closed.

Jones lay for a while in total immobility with the mild nausea of a man winded. He heard the whole broadcast right through, including the now-extended commentaries. This was the biggest news to have come out of the island in the twenty-five years he had lived here. He remembered how after that first dinner the Wazir had taken him to a corner, and he who throughout his career had kept reporters out of his Gulf began talking about a 'top-class journalist', actually stationed on the island, being 'a sight better for us than the garbled rubbish that gets fed to London via Cairo or Beirut, most of it emanating from Al-Bakr and his ilk'. He couldn't mean Jones himself – that was unthinkable: but the wide-eyed look he got from Romy, just in earshot beyond the sofa, told of her gay bewilderment at the sudden conversion Jones had seemingly wrought.

He put out his shaky fingers to turn the dial of his radio to the local frequency. It was playing European music from a half-forgotten era. He recognised 'Roses of Picardy' and then 'The Eton Boating Song'. The music stopped in mid-bar for an announcement in Arabic which he supposed was about the curfew. The newsmen in the Darwish, it was obvious, would have the whole story: some would surely have filed by now – that young weasel from Reuters, for instance; and Sandy McCulloch, who strung for AP. They would be all over the London papers in the morning. And the TV screens that very evening, quite probably, would be filled with the face of that Rivers, pontificating over his dangling charms.

His own professional shame now gave way to grief. His old friend was surely dead: the fiction of the 'Regency' was a palliative, a soft landing for ordinary people who admired him or even loved him, and certainly needed him; simple folk needed kings and rulers beyond whom there is no authority but God, whatever ancestral brigand had been first of the line. The Emir was the same age as himself. He had striven so to make sense of all that had overtaken his little country. He didn't deserve to be murdered by that glib and cocky boy of his. Jones found himself praying for his old man's soul, he who believed in neither souls nor prayers.

How, exactly, would the Emir have died? A sudden knife? Any islander could get an audience. Once recently the Emir had told Jones of his Diwan's complaints – ' "Emir, why you let any person come to you? Why you not let me decide who will see you?" I reply to my Diwan, "The strong will see me whether you say yes or whether you say no. So your no will prevent only the weak, who need me more than the strong." '

He had exchanged his sarong for trousers, took his canvas hat, and drove very slowly towards the Darwish. The engine was unusually loud in the deserted lanes of the old town. Shops were open, he supposed by order, but few were buying. At the major crossroads troops stood in tight fidgety groups: Jones spotted the insignia of the neighbouring republic from which, injudiciously, the old Emir had lately been persuaded to invite a training unit for his own small army, for the sake of 'Arab solidarity'.

The Darwish stood back isolated on its spit of land. Jones pulled up at a line of rocks across the road. Immediately, an overwhelming voice turned the whole air against him. From the road-block thirty yards ahead, at the start of the hotel's upward-sweeping approach, a loudspeaker was trained on him.

'*Barra assayara.*' Get out of your car.

He did so.

41

The great voice rasped, this time in English, 'Who ahr you?'

'Jones.'

His own voice was pathetically weak and could nowhere near span the distance.

He stood there in his canvas hat with his arms out in an attitude not of suppliance but exasperation.

'Jones,' he called again. 'Inglisi.'

The sun was in his eyes. He was imprecisely aware of uniformed men and vehicles drawn up ahead. He mistrusted all uniforms.

'Come forrward,' the loudspeaker menaced.

He walked stiffly into the sun towards the road-block. When he got there he discovered at once: though manned by soldiers from the island, a pot-bellied foreign captain from the neighbouring republic's so-called training unit was in command.

Jones ignored him. He addressed himself instead to the single officer present from the island's army, a young two-pipper. He gently explained that he required to visit the Darwish to collect his mail and send a telex. This lieutenant replied to him with nervous gruffness. He had orders, he said – trying not to let it seem that he was all the time aware of the foreign captain – that no one may enter or leave the hotel and that all telex machines were out of bounds. (In the hotel, Jones thought, Shark's-tooth Rivers and his whipper-snapper friends would be buzzing around like bluebottles in a jam-jar.)

Jones courteously enquired of the young man his name, and when he swiftly mentioned a kinsman known to him the man's gruffness changed to furtive humour.

'And from whom did your orders proceed?' Jones sought to know.

'From the palace. His Highness has made a proclamation.'

Jones felt dizzy in the fierce sun. Every fidget and twitch signalled, through the corner of his eye, the disapproval of the captain beside them. 'Have you seen it?' he pressed gently.

The captain could hold back no longer. 'It is not your business, Mister. Every unit has a copy. *Shuf!*' He withdrew from his shirt pocket a folded sheet of paper. Jones's eye turned on the man lazily. He took the paper with slow distaste and opened it up. It was a photostat of a document in Arabic with an English translation, erratically typed beneath, which read, 'In the name of Allah. In the light of my failing health and high age, I have appointed my son, the prince Hatim bin Ahmed Al Asnan as my Regent until my death to whom all obey. In the name of Allah.'

The Arabic above, which was also typescript, was signed with the familiar signature and stamped with the royal seal. All manner of document could be mocked up with a photocopier.

He did not stay to argue. You can't argue with the muzzles of guns. The hours immediately following a *coup d'état* were trigger-happy ones: it was like a fever with a predictable chart of high danger in the early phase. So many over-eager newsmen had been casually shot on account of choosing the wrong moment to push their luck. His shadow fell before him on the dusty tarmac as he walked back, and he thought all the way, what a fine clean target in the sun his back must be making for pot-belly's chubby little pistol.

He clambered into his elderly Packard, executed a clumsy turn and moved off with much noise the way he had come, wondering where he should go. It was fair to assume that Hatim's forces had control of all hotel and all external communications except a few short-wave diplomatic radios (the diplomats would be cowering in their compounds and seldom knew a damn thing anyway). They had cut all telex links: that could be done with the flick of a switch. He guessed they had disconnected only specific telephones, such as his, since they would need the telephone system themselves. But they would have routed all international dialling codes through their own operators. The journalists would stay under guard until the new regime was firmly in place and reversal from within unfeasible. A black-out on all information except the junta's 'official' line would prevent the Emir's neighbouring monarchies, operating with the tacit approval of America and Britain, from justifying intervention.

It was the standard *coup d'état* package. A façade of legitimacy had been quite skilfully run up. Very likely they had displayed the document of abdication with the Emir's signature on television: this could have been picked up on the mainland and wirephotoed to London and the rest of the gullible world.

He chugged slowly in high gear past the entrance to the port which was sealed by two full platoons of troops and here too (he could see) commanded by foreign republican officers. The town appeared cowed, the desert infiltrating the streets; and two lean dogs had entered this emptiness in a fast guilty lope along the strip of shade of the mainstreet banks which should have been open for the evening stint but were manifestly shut. If there had been any shooting, it had all finished now. From time to time military vehicles came by at high speed. A few soldiers, as if to invite hostility, were posted at the entrances of government buildings. He pulled up at the supermarket patronised by the expatriate community. About half the staff were present and fewer customers than staff. An English bank manager's wife spotted him thankfully and asked him if it was true the Emir was dead, and when he told her that he knew no more than she, and probably less, she looked aggrieved and alarmed at the same time, as if he had deliberately pushed her off his life-raft. An Indian department manager, who had omitted to change his shirt, whispered fearfully that mortar firing had been heard from the oil town and a power cut had brought part of the town to a standstill. Jones bought two tins of evaporated milk.

The Emir's palace lay beyond the old town where he lived. He wanted to stop and eat some cereal and make a cup of coffee, for he was feeling weak and persistently dizzy and he needed to sit down quietly and consider what he should do. He pulled up outside his home, but did not turn off the engine. In his absence someone had splashed an Arabic slogan in red paint on the wall further down the street: he could not tell whether it was for or against. He put the car into gear and moved off again.

The Packard emerged from the maze of alleys and joined one of the approach roads leading to the roundabout opposite the palace gates. Three armoured personnel carriers were drawn up at the gates, and the whole length of the palace walls was lined with troops carrying machine-guns, one man every few paces. Two anti-tank guns covered the entrance.

44

The racket of Jones's car signalled its approach from far away. He drove slowly into the roundabout in his customary top gear, made a complete circle, and pulled up on the further side from the gates. He got out laboriously and walked downwind from the roundabout's fountain, which played merrily and gave him a light spraying, towards the guardhouse alongside the main gates. He carried nothing. If they shot him, he did not see what he had to lose. But being an old man, owning an aged car, was to his advantage: such a comical figure belonged so little to this world as to present no threat to those who wished to changed it.

He had long experience of guardhouses and the like. The best way of walking past those who might challenge you was to wear a slight smile and fix your gaze on the point you wished to reach, on no account hurrying or faltering or catching anyone's eye. In such a manner Jones strode straight past the knot of armed soldiers and entered the cool of the guardhouse. Even here he did not hesitate but moved directly through the crowded guardroom to the empty chair opposite a desk and sat down heavily. Behind the desk was seated a major, a foreign republican, chewing gum. Anyone observing Jones for a prolonged period that day would have observed a distinct but unemphatic acquisition of purpose in his stride over the last several paces of his progress.

He leaned forward with a large mottled hand, which the major took as expected, and announced in his primitive Arabic that he was Mr Jones, a friend of His Highness the Emir and His Highness Prince Hatim, who had come to visit His Highness the Emir.

The sort of smile that policemen give to children too young to fear them brought a certain light to the major's sallow, efficient face. He was not wearing battle kit like the rest but a military shirt tailored to emphasise the breadth of his shoulders, and a tie. Jones was aware that a tie could carry a person a long way in the Third World, involving a complex knot devised by the dominant civilisation; but it was too late now to redeem his own tielessness.

The smile went out. 'His Highness the Emir is not receiving

visitors,' the major informed him suavely in English and resumed chewing.

'Perhaps,' Jones said, 'someone could tell him that I called.' From the wallet in his shirt pocket he extracted a visiting-card. He took his time. In situations like these you allow the suspicious and potentially hostile plenty of time. To get the feel of you. To size you up and sniff you around, like a large strange dog. He repeated his name and passed the card across.

The major studied it, first the English, then the Arabic on the other side. He too was taking his time.

'You are of the press?'

'Of the press.'

'You wish to report the change of government? We have a copy here of the proclamation of the Emir Ahmed.'

Oh, he'd seen it, Jones said, and thanked him. He had merely called to see the Emir Ahmed as an old friend. He couldn't report anything. The telephones didn't work and the telexes were under guard.

'We know him, sir,' one of the island officers present observed in Arabic. 'He is known to the Emir.'

'Please sit,' the major said.

Jones was already sitting. The major rose and went outside with the card, and Jones glimpsed him through the window talking by radio from one of the personnel carriers.

Jones was glad to enjoy the air-conditioning. After a minute or two, sweet milkless tea came round on a puddly tin tray and Jones took a glass of it. A few minutes later the major returned with two soldiers. Jones thought that he was being arrested, though it surprised him.

'These men,' the major said with the same amused condescension he had greeted him with, but intensified now, 'will take you to the palace.'

Surprise or gratitude are not appropriate at moments like these and Jones showed neither. He trudged between the soldiers in the fierce heat across the palace's broad forecourt which he had first crossed a quarter of a century before in a moment of immortality. The construction firm of the overweening Stuart-Smith, with his violent handshake and quilted lips, had then only just completed the rebuilding of the palace on the old site. It was in an immoderate Mogul style and faced with brown marble, in which Jones now noticed a bullet chip not there before.

They entered by a small door tucked in beside the imperious main steps, evidently used for the comings and goings of palace staff. The door gave on to a long passage flanked by administrative offices. At one of them Jones was delivered to a young officer of the island's forces who dismissed the escort and offered Jones a seat in an armchair, the room's only furniture. A strip light fluttered angrily from the ceiling like a dicky heart. Immediately the man began to harangue Jones, in English, on the island's happy fortune at the turn of events. 'The old Emir,' he assured his visitor from a standing position on the wall-to-wall carpet, 'was maybe adequate for the past, but today the past is finished. Am I correct? Today we people have reached the modern era, the era of the people themselves. This is what we believe in!' He spoke with the supercilious zeal of a senior pupil designated to initiate a new boy in the dubious glories of a third-rate school. 'The English will understand since you are a democratic people,' he added.

'Yet I have come to see His Highness, the Emir Ahmed,' Jones said clearly. He knew well that the young man had no brief to preach at him. 'That is all I've come for.'

'Yes, I know very well what you have come for. You will wait here, please.'

The young man turned abruptly and left the room, locking the door. It was cool: the palace air-conditioning had not faltered. Although curtained along one wall, the room had no windows. A coloured photograph of the Emir had been taken down from its hook on the wall and was leaning in its frame across a corner. The photograph was fifteen years old, Jones knew, but the shrewd eyes and buzzard's nose were characteristics that had lasted the course with the Emir into old age. The closely trimmed beard betrayed – it was said deliberately, as the mark of a charmed life – the ancient scar along the left side of the jawline: twenty-eight years ago a bullet had grazed him when a half-brother challenged his right to the succession.

It was unreasonable to suppose the old man was not already dead. He hadn't far to go himself, but he was sad that his old friend was probably gone ahead of him.

The photograph began to swim before Jones's eyes – it was omitting to eat, he could tell, that made him so light-headed.

He wasn't at all afraid. The very first time he had entered this palace that Stuart-Smith had built he was immortal, as he remembered, and something of that immortality invariably returned whenever he re-entered it. He had come for his first interview with the Emir, which had been arranged for him by Romy's father, and which Romy herself had tried to stop. She had telephoned him at the old Darwish early the previous evening. He had hurried down from his room in his sarong to take the call on the telephone on the high desk of the Greek manager in the dark entrance hall, because it was the only telephone there was – old-fashioned even for those days: one of the pedestal telephones with a daffodil mouthpiece.

A very cold voice. 'I hear my father has arranged for you to interview the Emir.' And she proceeds to threaten at once. 'But since you have already seen Al Bakr . . .' Suddenly she stops, as if she has forgotten her lines.

Jones is quite taken aback. He wasn't to know how cold her voice could be.

'I haven't seen the person you mention,' he says. 'As a matter of fact.'

'What?'

'I said I have not actually seen the individual you refer to.'

Now Romy, with menace: 'Since you *intend* to see him, *I* intend to tell my father who I have no doubt will advise the Emir to cancel your interview with him.'

'You do.'

'I do.'

'Providentially or not,' Jones pursues, composure re-asserting, 'I have not been able to locate this gentleman you referred to. So you may take it that I shall not be seeing him.'

'I see,' she says, but tugging against her own believing him.

Then he turns it round on her. 'There was something *I* wanted to talk to *you* about.'

'Go ahead.' A different sort of voice. A perceptible softening.

'I think not on the telephone.'

There is a pause. 'Perhaps tomorrow,' she says.

'There's not much opportunity. I'm on the afternoon flight to Beirut. You'll be at your dig.'

'What are you suggesting, then?' Her voice has been shifting up, up from the cold dark, like a diver ascending.

'Now.'

'I'm about to take Richard to the airport.' He remembers Richard Fenton from the dinner the previous night, the weedy diplomat, a stale suitor he supposed, of many years' lingering.

'Is Richard going somewhere?'

'Your mind is working like lightning.'

'After dinner then,' he proposes, casually urgent. 'A cup of coffee.'

'I suppose I could try. Something to do with seeing the Emir tomorrow?'

'Certainly not.'

'It's something special?' Yet another colour of voice. Vulnerable, in the diffused sun of the rising swimmer.

Something special? Something stupendous, unprecedented, something never before conceived of.

'I suppose you could call it that.'

He still remembered how slowly he lowered the earpiece on to its cradle. Some passages of a man's life are etched ineradicably. He had heard it said that in the end only the wounds are remembered. Yet there are wounds and wounds.

He was sleepy now in the sealed room. He dropped off. But he did not dream of Romy.

He was woken by a key in the lock. He did not know at first where he was. He had dreamed that he was flying his own light aircraft from an extreme northern island base on which only he was stationed, and he had made a discovery of a new land of exquisitely green ice cliffs and pinnacles, a land whose incomparable beauty awaited him if only he could let go whatever it was that isolated him in his 'singularity'.

'My dear Mr Jonas.'

This was a new young officer, roly-poly, full of lather.

'His Highness, the President-Regent, sends his most sincere apologies for keeping you waiting. He expresses very sincerely these apologies, and is now awaiting most impatiently to see you. Please.'

Jones was reluctant to move. He had been peculiarly at peace in his dream and he remembered the train of recollection that had preceded it, how in the course of two or three minutes the graph of Romy's voice had swept from a depth of cold disgust to the very surface of admitted love. Somehow that brilliance of love incorporated this palace itself, in that within a matter of hours the Emir, right here, by perceiving that he could trust this English journalist, had by this simple implication of his heart given to them his pontifical blessing. Therefore it was the Emir alone he desired to see, alive or even dead, not any plausible murderous son.

Nevertheless he found himself ushered out of the room from behind, directed along the passage, and up some stairs and through a door that gave suddenly on to the main great marble atrium. From here his effusive guide (an aide-de-camp, it was growing clear) led him, with a bit of a swagger, into a high-ceilinged stateroom whose shutters were closed and candelabras blazing. Only at this point did they pause, and here, from another room beyond, a tall, youthful Arab figure, in a black gold-hemmed gown of gossamer wool over a crisp white *dishdasha*, strode in.

Hatim held his hand out and with it, young hand clutching ancient hand, drew Jones like a valued emissary, long awaited, in a progress reeking of falsity, towards a pair of armchairs backed across a corner of the damasked walls.

He must go through with it now, whatever else.

The visitor conceded that, yes, it must be three years. (He remembered Hatim callow; in the three years he had acquired slime.)

'And now you come to call upon my poor father. That I am aware of, Mr Jones. But since we are fortunate enough to have you here, perhaps we may take this opportunity to give you a little briefing, a little background. Off the record!'

There was some flaw, Jones perceived, in the manner in

50

which Arab fathers raised their sons, that induced a tendency to patricide. As children they made them cosseted manikins, but thereafter wouldn't let them grow to be themselves. This Hatim was much like his father when younger, lean and beaky, with a close-trimmed beard. Yet somehow was grown crooked, the urbanity a cover, and the mouth too soft and cold.

'You have of course heard of the constitutional developments?'

Jones was looking about for signs of a fracas. For the first time in his life it occurred to him why chairs in Arab palaces were invariably backed against the wall.

'Something of the kind.'

'You saw the signed proclamation, Mr Jones?'

'I saw a photostat of something.'

'You must see the original, my dear fellow. You must see the original. Mohammed Abdu, can you please fetch –' and Hatim broke off into a moment's Arabic. 'Forgive me' – turning back to Jones with concern on his brow – 'in a minute, you will see, perhaps two.

'Now,' he resumed, to indicate the start of serious business. 'It is important that the *Post* receives the full facts, for what the *Post* presents as news the world knows as *facts*. Facts are sacred – yes! There is so much untruthful reporting, isn't it so? In London I always read the *Post*. That is my custom. It is something I have most specially missed since – since I returned to my homeland. Of course my father and I have not always seen eye and eye on the policy. But it was only to please the old men, the ulema you know, that he placed me for a while in restriction. It was not for me to object.' He opened his hands magnanimously. 'It has been so difficult for the old men and the religious elders to come to terms with the situation of today. Of course you believe in God, Mr Jones . . .'

Hatim waited. He saw an old man's dog eyes looking at him, telling him nothing.

'Mr Jones?'

It was a sort of question, Jones perceived, of sudden and unwarranted intimacy, which in this young man's mouth had become indecent.

'When I listen to music I do,' he said.

Hatim frowned. 'Of course you believe in God, and so do I. But alas, it is not God, much as we would both wish it, who controls the forces of international politics and the world economy. When the power was with the few, the monarchs and so on, it might have been possible to believe that the final authority lay with God. Believe me, I have studied the theory of the divine right of kings, studied it very fully. But today the power is with the masses, and today it is not reasonable to suppose that God is Prime Minister.'

At such spontaneous wit the speaker could not refrain from chuckling. He checked himself.

'Mind you,' he resumed, 'the power of the people is a moral power, and that power possesses the approval of God. Correct? In time, the ulema and their friends will come to realise it yet, mark my words.'

A low distaste had spread across Jones's face. His mottled hands lay folded and heavy in his lap. Hatim's words oozed and eddied around him like a backwater that accumulates detritus.

'My father has had a difficult furrow to plough, especially of late. His advisers were all old men, bearing the attitudes of the ancestors. My father himself knew that things must change. From time to time he would comment so to me, in the past. He was not blind. Far from it. But he had no opportunity to act.'

He shook his head, dissolving his regret in the magnificent rug across the marble floor.

'Inevitably it fell to us to act, as the people's will took shape. There was so much unrest: as an experienced reporter with your ear to the ground you will know better than I. At the docks, among the petroleum industry workers. Even the schools! When my father felt obliged to accept the advice to close the Asnan School, built to educate the next generation of the leaders of our people . . .' The affront of it halted him. 'It became our duty to act. To save the nation. Of course you see that.'

'Of course,' Jones echoed dully. His rheumy eyes, blue with age, regarded the puppy face. What could the boy have *done* with the old man?

'Money is one thing,' Hatim had resumed. 'We have enough

money. But you can bankrupt a people's *soul*. We had no choice. No choice at all. For my father's sake too. Naturally, the action taken was not instantly comprehended by everyone. Certain members of his entourage were unwise enough to open fire at the party which accompanied me here this morning to explain to my father the action which was necessary. My men were obliged to defend themselves, and in so doing my poor father was slightly injured in the shoulder by a stray bullet. The injury is slight – his doctor is of course with him – but nonetheless it has been a shock to him. That is why, when you see him, I want you not to tire him, to remain with him, I propose, three minutes only.' The brow furrowed and the narrow mouth smiled.

Jones gave a little nod. He felt stiff and sick. Where had they cornered him? At prayer? In the bathroom? In bed?

'It will reassure him to see you, Mr Jones.'

'Reassure him of what?'

'You will want to ask him, I expect, to confirm in person the contents of his proclamation – ah, you have the original, Mohammed Abdu.'

The aide was at hand to pass across a sheet of thick white palace writing-paper which trembled in Jones's fingers. It was indeed a single, undoctored document, bearing the Emir's authentic signature in ink.

'Fortunately my father's injury is in the left shoulder.' The Prince patted his own shoulder. 'You will wish to confirm the proclamation,' he pursued with his clammy smile. 'You will wish to confirm that apart from this injury he is alive and well. I have requested that his doctor shall be present when you visit so that he can explain to you the injury. You will, I expect, wish to ask my father if he has any message for our people at this turning-point in our history. And, of course, for the outside world. We are an important country now.' He sighed lightly. 'It is our destiny. You English have known what it is to be an important country.'

He inclined towards Jones, still not quite sure of his full attention.

'I don't expect you will want to ask my father anything more.

53

Your visit will tire him. If you have any questions, you may wish to ask me now.' And now he leaned back, cupping his hands as at prayer, ready for the probing interrogation of the international press.

Jones wondered what he should ask him. Where was the purpose in putting questions? His own left shoulder ached. All he wanted was to see the Emir, one old man and another. He hadn't come here for this. What possible use could it be? He had had enough of interviews.

The young man turned to him humouringly, as if to say, Must I supply you questions as well as answers? Has it come to this?

'What role is your brother to play?' Jones enquired wearily.

'My brother?'

'Yes.'

'We have sent our emissary to Texas to explain the situation to him.'

'But what role will he play?'

'We hope he will perhaps represent our country abroad. He will want to serve his country.'

'You mean, he is not to return here.'

'It is for him to decide himself, Mr Jones.'

'Where is Fuad Al-Bakr?'

'My Prime Minister? He is this afternoon addressing a meeting of petroleum workers at the oil town. Tonight we shall finalise the formation of his cabinet.'

'Who will be in the cabinet?' The questions were coming now of their own accord; a comic slipping into an old routine.

'The cabinet? I could not possibly say. It is too early.'

'I noticed that a foreign officer was in command at the gate here. The foreign soldiers are much in evidence in the town.'

'Are they? But they are our people's friends. Their officers and the sergeants and so forth were invited here by my own father on a mission to train our men. It is natural they should assume their share of responsibility at a time of – of potential challenge to the constitution.'

'Who is challenging the constitution?'

'I said "potential", Mr Jones. There is no challenge. The people's will is clear.'

'No arrests?'

'No arrests as such. A few old men are in custody for their own protection.'

'The Diwan, for instance . . .'

'One cannot be specific at this stage. You will understand this. It is still what we call "early days".'

'And your oil policy: do we expect any change?'

'My country, Mr Jones, as you know well, has been generously endowed by nature, you might say by God. You have lived here almost as long as I. But wealth thus granted must not be squandered. We have perhaps been helping to oversupply the world with petroleum. It may be that the new government will need to adjust the policy.' He paused and waited. 'You are ready now?'

Hatim rose with the merest rustle.

'Have you a pen?' He frowned pityingly at his visitor: a reporter without a pen! He snapped his fingers and his aide produced a gold ball-point pen. 'With my compliments,' Hatim said. '*Please*. And paper.' He reached to a low table of garish verdite for a memorandum pad. 'Now!'

He led the way from the corniced chamber. The aide followed.

They took the right-hand sweep of the broad marble staircase and at the top passed through a doorway where a soldier was posted, in crumbling shoes, a machine-gun at his hip. The broad corridor turned sharply left. They passed a room from which Jones heard the buzz of a telex machine.

Two young officers with revolvers stood outside a door on the left. Opposite, in the passage, a table bore an array of medical equipment and bottles, mostly, Jones supposed, for the sake of medical swank. One of the officers stepped forward and stood before Jones, who interpreted the movement and stood there like a penguin for the man to pat his way down his body from armpits to ankles, then up his legs to the crutch.

'A formality,' Prince Hatim lied. What broken symbol did these usurpers suppose they were protecting?

55

Taking a key from his pocket Hatim unlocked the heavy door and led Jones into a shuttered, lamplit bedchamber.

The figure lying there yellow and shrunk and swathed, on a low bed, propped by pillows, was not immediately recognisable. There was a smell of sterilised decay. Of course, it could be none other than the Emir, but Jones had never seen him like this before, never before without his head-cloth, his airy gown, his courtly bearing. His first thought was of a famous old movie star he had interviewed years and years ago, with his wig off, and little watery eyes peering at him out of holes in the crêpy skin.

The Emir's eyes were on him now, then moved to his son, then back to Jones, whom he now accorded a slow silent inclination of the head. The eyes betrayed nothing, not even recognition; they were sunk into the dark yellow corpse-face like sucked black pastilles.

The natural white of his beard, customarily dyed, was visible beneath the earlier blackened growth. A brocaded skull-cap topped his head and he wore a cotton nightshirt of which one side was slit to accommodate bulky bandaging of the shoulder and upper arm. A brown blob stained the bandaging and the arm was strapped to his side.

Beside the bed a middle-aged Punjabi occupied an armchair.

'Highness,' Jones said.

'Ah, Jonas,' the Emir responded feebly. 'How good of you to come.'

'I am glad to see your Highness alive.'

'It is true we are both alive, *hamd'ul illah*. Will you sit, Jonas? Here on the bed.'

There was nowhere else. A skinny right hand emerged from under the bedcover to motion Jones to his side, and scuttled back again. By the time Jones had begun to approach the bed itself, and to settle down on it, the distinction between himself and the other had become uncertain and the illusion supervened that the recumbent swaddled figure was himself.

The Emir went on ignoring his son (always the favoured child) who watched from the rug in the centre of the half-dark chamber.

'I'm afraid I've not come in a tie or a coat,' Jones murmured.

'I too,' the Emir concurred, 'am not in correct dress, I think.'

Here the doctor – the Punjabi – broke in hurriedly, as if rehearsed. The patient had a flesh wound. A projectile had entered beneath the collar-bone and left the body grazing the shoulder-blade. Only grazing, mind you. There had been some bleeding, naturally. The patient had taken a sedative, and must not be tired. Visitors must be very brief.

The Emir waited for the man drily. 'You find me as I would not wish to be found exactly,' he said.

Once again Jones was unexpectedly short of something to say.

'You have much to do, Jonas.'

'I may not stay long.'

'You have seen the proclamation.'

'It seemed to be your signature.'

'Ah, yes. I signed it of course. You saw that.'

An odd-shaped silence ensued.

'Your Highness,' Jones began, making a point of the honorific. He gathered his wits. 'How are you?'

'We have grown old together, Jonas. You and I are too old to fear to die.'

Jones searched his mind for a question. The blank pad was in his left hand and the pen in his pocket. He was cross with himself for running out of questions so soon.

'Perhaps you have a message for your people, and the outside world.'

'My people?' The old man seemed to strain for recollection. 'They are in my thoughts. I wish them well under . . . under . . .' – his eyes crawled towards the figure of his son but not to his face – 'the present government.'

'And the international community?'

'Ah, yes. Our friends must accept that we must . . . resolve our problems in our own way without interferences.'

Another silence fell, closing them off. The doctor made an ugly officious purse of his lips. Jones supposed he should make a note and glanced at the blank pad. 'Is there anything else you wish to say, Highness?'

The Emir looked back at his son, this time slap into his face.

'There is my son,' he said carefully. 'He is the one with the right to wish. I am in the hands of Allah, in whom we all must trust, Jonas.' For the second time God had been invoked for them jointly.

'Then I will leave Your Highness to rest.'

'We old men need rest, do we not? You will shake my hand, Jonas. We have known one another so long, in varying circumstances.'

The crabbed hand again crept from the bedclothes. It tightened round Jones's hand awkwardly as if to keep him there. Jones felt some tiny thing pressing the centre of his palm: and the Emir's hand twisted so that Jones's palm was beneath. Something was being passed to him. Jones held the thing against his palm by the ball of his thumb. He supposed it to be a screw of paper. He felt Hatim's eyes upon them. He stood. As he walked past Hatim to the door he transferred it to his trouser pocket. He wished to say something that hinted of his loyalty, but he couldn't think of how to put it.

Hatim locked the door behind them.

Jones moved down the corridor by the way they had come. 'Mr Jones,' Hatim said behind him.

Jones stopped. He turned slowly.

'Yes?'

Hatim faced him with an expression close to a sneer.

'You have seen for yourself,' he said. 'My father is quite well.'

'Yes, of course.'

'He would like the world to know.'

'I have no means of sending a dispatch.'

Jones turned away. He could not attempt to mask his disgust.

'Major Mohammed Abdu here,' Hatim said, 'will conduct you to a typewriter. Then he will arrange to telex your dispatch. And here –' they had reached the main stairs – 'I will say goodbye. And congratulate you on your "scoop".'

He confronted Jones squarely, holding out a hand as if to trump his father's. But to Jones, the hand that he took might have been a snake's head.

*

58

He had walked into this: he had only himself to blame. He was long past it, of course – he would never have got himself cornered like this in the old days. If he refused to write anything, what could they do? Keep him here? Lock him up? Throw him off the island? The place was finished for him anyway. So was he: he had nowhere else to go . . .

The plump aide's soft hands had cajoled and fluttered him into an office where a large upright Remington manual typewriter stood on a desk. It surprised him they had nothing more modern. White paper was brought, and carbon. It was fed for him into the roller. He felt like a little boy who if he refused his rice pudding would be presented it every mealtime until he got it down. How could he write what they wanted from him without his vomiting? It would clog his gullet. It would be the last dispatch he would ever write. It would finish him. If he were a child he would cry and stamp.

Did it still matter? he wondered.

The aide had got him up to the desk and was nuzzling a swivel chair against the back of his legs. What could he write? He sat down and typed that the Emir Ahmed al-Asnan had seen him in audience (he did not write 'private') following his abdication in favour of his son Hatim, and although slightly injured by a bullet in the shoulder, made a statement. He then quoted the Emir's words accepting the authority of his slimy son and endorsing the proclamation he had signed. The dispatch was like a death-warrant on all that the island had always meant to him, but strangely he could not get the significance of this death-warrant through to himself. He read it through two or three times. It *was* a sort of death-warrant but the magnitude of his betrayal still eluded him, either because it was altogether too vast or else because it was of no consequence at all. He knew he could pull it off the roller and screw it up into a little ball and hand it to the aide like a turd. But he didn't. He couldn't or he wouldn't, he did not know which. Instead, he typed the telex number and the usual dateline and the time slug at the top, and he turned the roller back and ended it with the words BUST BUST REGARDS, JONES. P.S. I AM NOT REPEAT NOT IN REACH OF THE TELEX TRANSMITTING

The aide fidgeted about in the room, impatient to pull the dispatch off the machine. When he had the single page in his hands he read it with ponderous concentration.

'Mr Jonas,' he began, suddenly ominous.

Jones looked up.

'Excuse me. I think this is rather short.'

'It is all I have to report.'

'You do not report of the purpose of the new Government. You do not discuss the new Prime Minister, Mr Fuad Al-Bakr.'

'Prince Hatim was talking to me off the record, Major. I cannot move freely around the town. I can only write of the interview with His Highness the Emir.'

'The father of the President-Regent.'

'As you wish.' Jones rubbed his eyes with the back of his hand. He had had enough of this. 'It is all there is to write,' he repeated dully. 'I have nothing more to offer you.'

The major scrutinised the text again. ' "The former Emir said his people were in his thoughts," he read aloud, ' "and he wished them well under the present Government." Is it correct – "his" people?'

'He hasn't any others, Major.'

'Then, tomorrow the people of England will know the truth, yes, Mr Jonas?'

'They might,' Jones said. These Arabs hadn't grasped the fact that the *Post* did not publish on a Sunday. There would be a duty man in the newsroom, some dolt on overtime. The *Post* wouldn't go to press again for another twenty-four hours.

'Excuse me, Mr Jonas. Why you write "bust bust regards"? – You mean "best best regards".'

'Funnily enough, I don't. "Bust bust regards" is how we end messages at the *Post*. It's a way of saying "no more for now" and "goodbye" at the same time.'

'Like that – "bust bust regards"?'

'Odd, isn't it? Why don't we take it to the telex operator?' Jones proposed. He wanted to assess the danger of the man on duty being familiar with Fleet Street cablese. 'Bust bust' meant 'cancel'.

'I shall take it.'

'My message will not be altered?'

'No one must interfere with what a journalist shall write from here. It would be against the principles of freedom of information. Only if the message was not accurate.'

'But that is accurate.'

'It seems accurate. Please wait.'

The aide disappeared with typescript, effusiveness displaced by uncertainty. Jones surmised the dispatch was being put before Hatim. The words 'bust bust' could, he supposed, cost him his life. He'd done it as a sort of joke at the last moment.

Five minutes later the aide returned, primed again with cheer, and chattering about the hot weather escorted Jones down the main stairway.

'Mr Jonas,' he announced on the palace steps, 'you are our friend. Call back whenever you like. Whenever you like.'

Jones had the palace forecourt to cross first.

He walked towards the gates very slowly so that if someone had rumbled the meaning of the words 'bust bust' they could summon him back and lock him up or shoot him at once. He would feel a comfort, going out under the same roof as the old Emir. If he was to be shot, he would prefer the palace. He had a most idiosyncratic distaste for obscurity, he was aware of that.

He was looking at the fat holster on the thigh of the soldier at the gates when all of a sudden the soldier became agitated. He and a fellow had sprung into lively expectation of an imminent happening. They were about to open the main gates. For Jones? Yet he could leave by the little pedestrian gate at the guardhouse. The soldiers were trotting with the long arc of the main gates as they swung them open. And here was an armoured car approaching at speed, and behind it a white Mercedes.

As the two vehicles swept into the forecourt the soldiers saluted. Jones was only a yard or two from the gates then. He caught sight of the occupant in the back of the Mercedes: a black-and-white chequered head-cloth, and beneath it a familiar bespectacled ill-bred face. For a moment the passenger's eyes met Jones's, but then the car had gone by . . . yet not quite so fast-motion a replay of ancient glances as to have denied Jones and Al-Bakr the stab of recognition.

So Jones left by the main gates. And in that last stretch to his old car parked beyond the roundabout where the fountain danced, he felt a little surge of elation. He had made a fool of that pair of usurpers with his 'bust bust'. He had taken the trick.

He got into his old Packard and started up. As he moved off he switched on his cassette-player, and turned the knob to full volume so that even at the gate they would receive a distant blast of the Pilgrims March from the *Meistersingers*.

5

When he got home he went into the kitchen and opened a tin of evaporated milk. He sat down to a large plate of cornflakes. He brought the sugarbowl over from the sideboard and, when he spooned on sugar, agitated ants sprinted all over the table. After several mouthfuls, he opened a can of beer and drank directly from it. Then he put his right hand into his trouser pocket and felt around for the little screw of paper. It was there among his loose change. He opened it out under the light. It was only two inches square, torn from a flyleaf of a Koran, with a message written in ball-point in Arabic and difficult to make out. He recognised the Arabic signature of the Emir.

He glanced at his watch. One hour to curfew. They could come for him any time – inveterately idiots were employed on the Foreign Desk who, if telephoned at home, would tell the Saturday duty man to query the 'bust bust'. Either that or they would print the dispatch tomorrow for Monday. That would be dreadful. Of course, he didn't even know for certain whether the palace telex operator had transmitted the 'bust bust' verbatim: he had allowed himself to be ushered from the palace without asking for a copy of his own telex. He hadn't even brought out the carbon of his typescript.

The elation was quite gone now. He could see Al-Bakr strutting through the staterooms, and Hatim sliding across to tell him how he'd made a poodle of old Jonas.

He had lost his grip, he could see that: if he hadn't lost his grip he would never have let them persuade him to write anything at all. It seemed to him now so easy to have defied them and to have taken the consequences. He'd really rather they came for him right this minute and got it done with: somebody in the palace would know where he lived. They could wheedle it out of the Emir himself. Maybe if they didn't come now he could take himself back to the palace and somehow get to the telex machine on the pretext of adding to his dispatch and he could tell those fools on the Foreign Desk outright not to give that dispatch to the Back Bench, not on any account to print tomorrow for Monday.

He was the idiot, that was clear enough. It was just that he couldn't any longer bring himself to engage in heroics. He was too old for heroics: he was washed up – the slang was descriptive. He saw the old Emir, yellowed and cadaverous: it was as if they were lying there together on the tide-line, bleached and lifeless, halfway to becoming sea and sand.

Now that he couldn't live here on this island any more, he mused vaguely as to what he should do. He knew he had burned his boats – years and years ago he had burned his boats. Out of the vagueness, he identified the exact moment of boat-burning: when he handed the letter to the postman. It was a minuscule occurrence in itself – more like the moment when a heart chooses to stop. It began with his flying in to London from the Middle East without telling Liz and going straight from Heathrow to the dingy London bed-sit the *Post* let him keep on a fourth floor just off the Strand. A stray cat has got in and at the moment he opens the door the creature leaps to the top of the window and then out into the half-darkness and drizzle. He is just peering out into the well of the flats to see what happened to the cat when the telephone starts ringing.

He sits on the unmade bed to take it. It's the Foreign Editor saying, 'You've got to do something fast, dear boy.' Some fool on the Desk has called home asking to speak to him and of course Liz has answered not knowing he was due back. They said they thought the plane must have been late. Now here's the Foreign Editor telling him he didn't think Liz swallowed it. She'd be trying to ring him at the flat any moment now. 'If you've got your lady-friend there get her out quick.'

Jones is still in his tropical suit and his felt hat, with the unpacked suitcase and knocked-about portable with the remains of innumerable labels dumped in the threadbare armchair.

'What lady-friend?'

Romy's never been here.

'Oh Gran. Don't imagine all your *chers collègues* are deaf

64

and dumb. I hear she's a glittering lady, dear boy, some pro-consular offspring, right? I'm making no moral judgments. All I'm saying is, Pack her out of the flat and fast. It'll end in terrible tears.'

Jones reaches out a long hand to take a photograph from the mirror frame. It's a small black-and-white snapshot of Liz with the boys when they were about six and eight, beside a plastic paddling pool in the Lamarsh garden, grinning into his camera. The boys are virtually grown-up now.

The Editor wanted to talk to him about the Commonwealth PMs' conference, the Foreign Editor says.

'What about it?' Jones asks.

'They're all arriving in London next week.'

'Oh, is that all? A piece for tonight?' It is already four p.m.

'Tomorrow for Wednesday. They're going to try to throw out the South Africans. You'd better come in.'

'One was vaguely aware,' Jones says in the mock-languid way he had when he felt people trying to stampede him. 'Look, d'you suppose Liz has picked up anything?'

'I haven't any *evidence* she has, Gran. There's talk here, in the newsroom, I'm bound to tell you.'

'It hasn't been a marriage for years.'

He is looking at the snapshot in his fingers. Liz has just had her hair styled in a new way, without warning, a surprise for him on his return from somewhere.

'There are marriages and marriages, dear boy.'

'Nobody's stealing me away from Liz.'

'Whatever you say, Gran.'

When he rings off he does not hang up; instead he pushes the receiver under the rather greasy pillow to muffle the dialling tone. He tries to turn the knob of the radiator but it is too stiff. The cactus seems to have survived but the potted plant has died of thirst, dark and neglect. The room stinks of cat.

He partially unpacks his suitcase. Under a crumple of socks he finds a batch of receipts, and these he smooths and sorts out, setting aside the hotel receipts that are made out to 'Mr & Mrs Jones', or '2 pers'. He begins to burn these over the gas ring.

He sets up his typewriter on the cheap table. At a typewriter he can think. He types, 'Dearest Liz, I am best on paper and that's why the sad things I have to say are coming to you on paper.

'Gavin once said, "If you love Mummy, you would have given her a divorce" . . .'

He types in short paragraphs on white A4 paper in double spacing, like a dispatch. Tears well in his eyes and he gets up to pour himself a whisky in a tooth-mug. He reads it through carefully, correcting as he goes, and then he takes another sheet of A4 and laboriously copies out the whole letter in freehand. He glances at his watch because he wants to catch the post. He rummages about for an unused envelope, and finds one. It has the name of a Lebanese hotel on it, one that he and Romy have been to together, but it will have to do. He rereads the letter and seals it.

He emerges into the cold autumnal London gloom, then hurries back to fetch the raincoat from the back of the door and puts his telephone back on the hook. Now he has entered the foyer of the Charing Cross Hotel and asks the hall porter for a stamp. The porter asks if he may enquire his room number, and Jones explains he was just meeting someone here for a drink, which the porter shows he doesn't believe without actually saying so. Thus another minute or two are lost before the man reluctantly brings himself to sell a threepenny stamp to a non-resident.

Out in the station forecourt he casts about for a post-box. A GPO van is drawn up at a double pillar-box in the Strand which a postman is there and then emptying. Jones dashes across, but he is too late – the van has pulled away. He stands there in the near-rain. Then he sees the van held up at the lights into Trafalgar Square. He set off in pursuit at the double and hands the letter to the driver just as the lights are changing.

That was the moment of the burning of those boats. Liz stayed on in their house in Essex and, when she died of the brain tumour nobody even told him about, the boys shared the proceeds equally. He had no other home to go to now.

He didn't feel up to finishing his cornflakes. He glanced

down at the scrap of India paper. The ants were inspecting it. Would they not come for him after all? Everything was so quiet, even his parrot. The light was going.

He finished the beer and shuffled out of his front entrance and round to the entrance of the other half of the compound. He felt exposed standing in front of the solid iron gates ringing and ringing without response. Would they be watching him now, in any case? After fully two minutes the postern door set into the gates opened a fraction. Then it was drawn back quickly, and there was his servant Aziz, wide-eyed, gripping him by hand and wrist, dragging him in. Aziz reeked of fear.

Aziz conducted him into the *majlis*, a long dark chamber of alcoves, rugs and incense. It was cluttered with gadgets and gewgaws of foreign manufacture, all in execrable taste. His landlord Suleiman rose, lean, hunched, and wary. He was a cantankerous man at the best of times. The two men exchanged prolonged unhurried Arabic greetings and seated themselves on cushions on the floor. Half in English, half in Arabic, they mourned the turn of events. They warned one another of retribution at the hands of the new regime: police might call at any hour. Suleiman had word of the arrest of friends.

Only when Aziz brought them cardamom-flavoured coffee did Jones reveal that he had been to the palace, and how he had been admitted to the Emir and found him lying in his bed injured. His account was punctuated by little grunts of alarm and admiration from the back of his host's throat. Then he told how he had smuggled out a piece of handwriting bearing the Emir's signature. Suleiman's eyes narrowed upon his guest. Jones produced the scrap of paper.

The elderly merchant brought out his spectacles and required Aziz to bring up the lamp shaded with maroon and cream plastic segments. First he read in silence; his head gave a little nod, and he began to translate haltingly: '"In the name of the All-Compassionate. My hand was forced upon the paper which appointed my son Hatim in my place and that paper has no value in sight of God or man. Ahmed bin Turki al-Asnan. Emir."'

It bore that day's date by the hijra calendar.

He laid the scrap of paper on the hard velveteen cushion beside him and smoothed it carefully with his middle finger.

'If the people knew of this paper,' the merchant began thinly, then all at once was overwhelmed by inward ferocity, '*tonight* they would take the sword and the gun against Hatim! The soldiers would not obey the orders of Hatim!' It was all obvious, he continued. The common folk were in doubt as to what to believe: they had seen copies of the signed proclamation: it had been shown repeatedly on television: they lacked conviction to act. This paper would give it them!

Suleiman's eyes were ablaze. He was like a single tree in a still landscape, struck by a squall. He lifted the fragment from the cushion and shook it in his fingers. Eddies of this wind began to reach Jones. He could perceive that this little message was enough to wipe out all the new regime's pretensions of legitimacy. The international community now had some justification to intervene if it chose, and it still might so choose. God, God, he cursed himself, let those fools in London not run his bust dispatch.

A torpor welled from his depths. He, Jones, should make a move. But what? What could he do? If he were to send a genuine dispatch he would have to reach the mainland. A man might get there by boat, he supposed – but the port was closed.

He started to try to explain it to his old neighbour. Could Suleiman organise a *boum* to put in to the creek on the south side? Apart from the port itself, it was the only place sufficiently deep to bring in a boat big enough to reach the mainland. Only a few fishermen lived at the creek. Jones could avoid the roads: he knew his way by the tracks in the dunes – at least he supposed he still did. Could they watch the whole coastline?

Suleiman regarded him sullenly. 'You must leave the paper for me, Jonas.'

Had the man understood nothing of what Jones had been saying?

'*I* shall need it, Suleiman.' Anyway it was not Suleiman's to keep. He alone had the right to the paper.

The other glared. He still had the fragment in his fingers.

Jones told him he had understood nothing. He would explain

it all again. Moreover, he, Jones, must send a picture of the Emir's message by wirephoto – an image transmitted by the telephone line – through the local newspaper on the mainland. They'd certainly have such a machine there.

'What wirephoto, Jonas?' Suleiman demanded narrowly.

'The wirephoto transmitting machine which is how pictures from abroad reach newspapers. Unless people see the actual writing, the actual signature, they won't believe it. The other nations must be made to believe. They won't believe easily. The actual writing – that might convince them.'

'We must have the paper here, Jonas.'

'Certainly not.' The man was an ignoramus, a semi-barbarian. 'The Emir gave it to me.' If he tried to snatch it back, it could be damaged.

'His Highness the Emir,' Suleiman rasped, 'wrote the paper for everyone. How he know you will make the visit to him?'

'He entrusted it to me.'

'To the people,' Suleiman corrected him mulishly. Then he said suddenly, 'I will call my son.' He summoned Aziz at once to find his son.

'I must have the paper, Suleiman,' Jones said quickly. 'My dispatch will be useless without it.'

'My son will make copies. He has that machine.'

But it was this that tipped Jones into exasperation. He flared hot with anger. 'He bloody won't.'

Suleiman now turned cautious and sinuous.

'Why, Jonas?'

Why? Why? Because he was not going to have those whipper-snappers in the Darwish getting hold of a photocopy and somehow transmitting it or its contents before he had filed. Not over his dead body. But he left Suleiman's question unanswered. All he said was, 'You have a *boum* in port?'

'Perr-haps one which I can reach. Perr-haps.'

'It's a question of time, don't you understand? If I cannot send my dispatch by tomorrow, for publication the next day, it will be too late. Don't you understand?'

How could he understand, this poor savage? There was no sentiment in power politics. One *de facto* was worth a hundred

69

de jures. He had been in the business long enough to know. Most likely it was too late already . . . They sat in silence, the other still holding the paper. Only fifteen minutes to curfew. It was never wise to break a curfew the first day of a *coup*: the soldiery was invariably over-zealous and jumpy. If he was to be shot he wasn't going to let it ever be said that he was *inexperienced*.

Suleiman's son entered, busy, chubby, self-important, with fear all over him. Though breathless, he greeted his father with formality, and acknowledged Jones politely. Suleiman told him of Jones's visit to the Emir, of a possible requirement for a boat. The fear at once sharpened into alarm. The smooth brow took on a sudden rash of furrows and his glance jerked to and fro between father and guest. He gave vent to a rapid speech of objection in Arabic. The line of his argument, Jones discerned, was that what his father proposed could mean the downfall of the family; to lie low, do nothing, could preserve it.

Suleiman regarded his son with distaste. He told him he was unfit to carry his name. He would send for another son who had more than a girl's courage.

The son retorted that his father and Jonas were old men who had no life to lose. The Emir likewise: he had no right to make trouble.

Repeating the young man's last two words, Suleiman's wrath exploded. Jones thought he would rise and strike the boy, but the assault remained verbal. They were indeed now standing, confronting one another, the son – the taller – having risked his objection, now cowed and silent. Here was Jones's theory in action again – that an Arab never really grew up until his father was dead. The father led his son into the little paved garden, which Jones's wall cut off. The tone of their voices – the son beginning to assent – dropped to one of conspiracy. Jones saw Suleiman showing on the paper in the fading light. Then abruptly the young man left.

'Where has he gone with the paper?' Jones demanded.

'He is returning. Five minutes.'

'Where's he gone with it?'

'He will show it to my other son, who will find the master of the *boum*. *Insh'allah*.' Suleiman seemed perfectly calm.

'He is not to copy it.' A growl.

'Why, Mr Jonas?' the old Arab reiterated stubbornly.

Jones had thought of a good reason, now. 'If copies get around town, before the world has the facts, it would ruin everything. Hatim and Al-Bakr will put out a statement that they expect reactionary elements to forge documents in the name of the Emir. "Beware false documents", they will warn.' Fleet Street knew it as a 'pre-emptive disclaimer'.

'He is showing it to my son Fahad, to persuade him. That is all. Why should he copy? I have said my word!' he concluded petulantly.

'I need it at once, Suleiman. I must leave now.'

Jones saw the hands of his watch closing on the curfew deadline. In the silence he felt his heart like a sluggard in his body. He did not want to have to do any of this. If it fell to him, he supposed vaguely it would be the last thing he would ever do.

Then the young man re-entered and handed the fragment of paper to his father, who passed it to Jones.

'My sons will arrange the *boum*, *insh'allah*,' Suleiman announced. He smiled. 'Without, it is finish, *khalas*.' He took Jones's arm and led him affectionately to the door. They could switch mood in seconds, these Arabs. 'You, Jonas, are the friend of our people,' he announced proudly. The words were like those of the cheap aide, but this man spoke from the gut, and Jones smiled too: two ancient caverns letting the light in.

Jones said, 'Tell Aziz to look after my parrot.' He made a squawk.

As the merchant's iron door clanged behind him, calls to prayer broke out all over the city like air-raid sirens. The whole place was battened down and full of fear. He was turning the key in the lock of his own front door when the amplified muezzin of the little mosque immediately opposite burst forth like a personal warning of dread menace. There was not another soul in the narrow street, not so much as a dog.

An envelope had been pushed under the door. He bent to pick it up. As he read, a smile flickered once again. It was McCulloch, writing in frantic tones that he was under house

71

arrest, his telephone cut off, and could Jones stir the Embassy into action? The other newsmen were holed up in the Darwish unable to move or file.

He assembled his sarong, a razor, soap, a tooth-brush, a packet of Kensitas, his transistor radio, his passport, and water in a Kia-Ora bottle. The light in the patio was quickly disappearing. He glanced at the letter for Paul propped against the amphora. As he started to leave by the dark passageway to the front door, his ears were accosted by a tortured exclamation in Japanese, *Ee-oo-i oo-ah-ahahuh ay-oh*! which by phonetic alchemy could be traced to Shakespeare.

He turned back to the parrot's cage.

'Bye-bye, Trudi,' he said.

'Bye-bye, Trudi.'

She had not spoken for days. Most of her conversation had been taught by Romy, and *If music be the food of love, play on* was Trudi's feat.

He drove by backroads. The streets were blind. On the edge of the town the half-wild pack of dogs was assembling early for its nocturnal scavenge. As luck had it, he did not encounter a single soldier or military vehicle. The old Packard now nosed in among the maze of possible routes through the salty dunes of the southern littoral. The engine without its silencer was wildly rowdy but here it didn't matter. These dunes were uninhabited. He was driving without lights and darkness closed in on him like a windowless room that contained just him and his straining engine. Twenty years ago he had known all the ins and outs among the dunes. Now he felt quite uncertain. The creek was only eleven miles from the town but the ground had lost its features, a jumbled wasteland under the blackness. Ten m.p.h. was the maximum: there was no hurry now.

After four or five miles he guessed he had lost his direction. He was guiding the Packard through the clumps of saltbush and sea-grasses. The old car mounted a tussock and was brought up sharp. At once both drive-wheels spun. It was as if the car had read his uncertainty. He tried to rock it off, but the wheels were burrowing into soft sand. He got out and knelt beside one half-buried wheel, took out Hatim's gold pen and applied its tip to the valve pin. When he had released half the air first of one wheel, then of the other, he climbed back into the car, backed off the tussock and manoeuvred round it. Before he regathered speed, he caught the soft sand again; now the front bumper was up against clubbed roots, blocking him as the rear wheels spun. He didn't bother to inspect the wheels. He took his things out of the car, and leaving the doors unlocked began to walk.

He could see quite well now, and the swiftly risen moon guided him by its position at his left. He stumbled often, more than he considered necessary. He kept mistaking the height of the dune ridges and the density of the glaucous saltbush thickets which were ghostly in the moonlight but cast shadows like men. Low thorns and thistles tore his bare ankles. He welcomed the mild pain because it brought his body closer to him and sharpened him against his lightheadedness. The distance was greater than he recollected and he wondered if he was walking in a circle; but the moon was still where it should be. Soon rents began to appear in his trouser-ends, for the thorns were hard as claws.

When he first glimpsed ahead the infinite spectacle of moonlight on the waters of the creek, he felt sick with a sort of vertiginous fear. He saw Romy waiting for him and looking at him from some distance out there in the water. He walked on, over the last overhanging dune of the foreshore; as he came down the firm strand to wash his ankles and the little crabs scuttled agilely into the wave-edge before him, he noted the trembling of his legs and how oddly his heart was lolloping about inside him.

He had never returned since that day.

Nothing was left of Romy's onshore excavation, not a vestige of evidence that anyone ever dug here. Sand was always quick to reclaim its domain. The Department of Antiquities and Heritage had developed other sites since. The cable drum was still there, buried more deeply now; in its turn it would become an object for excavation. In immensely ancient times this creek had been a haven for ships plying the Gulf trade; the long-buried settlement here dealt in frankincense and limes and copper ore for bronze, and probably in ivory and gold, all those goods Romy had listed in the fish market. The *tel* mound she had uncovered was of such paltry elevation that it was the cable drum they came to take as their point of reference – so many yards up or down from the drum. When she began to dig, she found that the settlement spilled out beneath what was now the sea and that beyond it in the creek lay hewn stones that must have formed a harbour arm.

As he came out from the wave-edge, a wild dog ran up the shore and began to growl and bark at him monotonously. This set off a dog barking in the cluster of fishermen's palm-frond huts up-creek. He crouched behind the cable drum, lest anyone looked out and saw this tall European interloper, so late at night, in a place none visited nowadays. He could not be sure that this scattering of fishtrappers knew yet of the upheaval and the curfew. News had a way of travelling across open spaces . . . The main editions of the Sundays would be going to press in Fleet Street, their front pages locked up now. In an hour or so each of the night news editors would be receiving copies of their rivals' first editions by means of the time-honoured network of collaborators in the dispatch rooms. How much did any of them know?

He tried to pick up the BBC World Service on his transistor and chanced upon an exceptionally clear signal. When the news came up, the island's events were again the lead item. A Reuters report from the island was quoted, stating that the people had taken the news of the Emir's abdication quietly and that forces loyal to the President-Regent were in control of all parts of the island, but that the airport and normal communications were still closed. The new government under the premiership of Fuad Al-Bakr was expected to be announced early the next day. The *coup d'état*, though unexpected, was reported as 'entirely without bloodshed'.

It all seemed cut and dried, a *fait accompli*. He felt himself to be engaged on a worthless escapade. The smug young weasel from Reuters had evidently persuaded someone to let him move a helpful dispatch. Quite likely all the newsmen would be running about town in the morning. That puffed-up ignoramus from television would be concocting a film about the passing of a repressive regime and the dawning of the enlightened rule of the people. When the visiting journalists were gone the executions would begin . . . The broadcast told of Mid-Eastern anti-Western governments, plus the East European satellites, recognising the new regime. The familiar cynical bandwagonery. Jones knew that once the major Western powers conceded recognition, that would be that. The strutters and cheats would have it; the last heart would be out of common folk and what they always feared, that man was a cold race, would be shown true; there could be no more blessed threat of the Emir's friendly neighbours intervening, for the West would restrain them. If the fools in London were to print on Monday the dispatch he had tried to bust (and, God knows, fools they were), *he himself* would have helped tip Britain and America into recognition.

He was lying curled up right under the rim of the cable drum, to hide himself. He tried to sleep, but could not. After their initial panic the crabs ignored him and he could see them diligently pushing up little cones of sand as they excavated their burrows. Romy used to bait the crabs, dashing round to cut off their flight to the sea; they would stop and raise their claws in readiness for combat and she would imitate them, sparring with them. She was an ardent chaser and provoker of counter-pursuit, absurdly puppyish for her role in the community and her age. He would seldom let her catch him, yet *he* would always catch *her*: it struck him now, for the first time, that this was not because he could still outrun her but because she *allowed* him to catch her. When he caught her (if they were alone) as like as not they would make love, for something in the movement of her body in evasion prompted the assault of love. His energy for her never faltered: they loved like twenty-year-olds. Even at the time he wondered at it, this radical vigour. After Romy, he never wanted another woman. The need of women had gone out of him.

If she returned now, just as she was, would she have the power to kindle and blaze the primal energy? Early one morning – it cannot have been long after dawn – Jones woke to find her gone. He rolls out of their bunk, wraps his sarong around him, puts on his canvas hat and emerges from their palm-frond hut in the dunes just inland from the dig. Her Land Rover stands alongside. The excavation is well under way. The first sun is striking the sea.

It is low tide. The barge with the lifting gear is anchored just offshore, the crewmen still asleep. Wavelets break on the sand. Suddenly he sees her down the beach with wild fair hair flying, performing an outlandish war-dance in a petticoat. She is scampering along the waterline at a great rate, then turning to face up the beach with legs bent and feet apart like a desperate goalie, and her arms spread and hands turned into claws. He can hear her across the silence like a Samurai in combat, 'Hai! Hai!'

It is a crab-bait.

As soon as she sees him approach he too threatens her with arms raised like the crabs. She responds by fleeing from him, provoking him into pursuit, every now and then turning to challenge him with mock claws. He chases her into the shallows where he almost catches her, but she ducks away and he loses his hat. Then up the beach and into the dunes where he seems to have outpaced her, trapping her on her back in a hollow. They are both panting.

She looks up into his eyes with utter mischief.

'You're a poor old gentleman, Mister Jones,' she quavers.

Jones has her pinned to the sand by her wrists. He snarls wickedly.

'You're a poor . . .' she repeats, but he has begun to close her mouth with his. Her body makes one final and futile attempt to wriggle free but her mouth has turned traitor and in a moment all of her is lost to him.

Suddenly the sound of an approaching vehicle. Jones leaps to his feet.

'It's the Emir!'

Quick as fire she doubles back down towards the sea and out of sight of the intruders, and then beneath the lip of the dunes to the hut.

Jones brushes the sand from his sarong and forearms, and moves towards the approaching Land Rover, bumping over the rough track through the dunes. It is brand-new and flies the island's flag. The Emir sits beside the driver, with six-year-old Hatim on his knee. Two askaris, bodyguards, are in the back.

Jones welcomes the visitors gravely. The Emir announces, 'I have come to see the history Miss Romy has been digging from the ground. Miss Romy is here?'

Jones scans round, mock-puzzled. 'She was here a moment ago, Highness. She seems to have gone to ground.'

Everyone knew of the Emir's practice of rising early to tour his domain.

'Miss Romy will show me the history,' he announces.

Jones must play for time. He instructs the Land Rover with its passengers to follow, and processes ahead along the remains of the track, detouring first for one of his sandals, then for another, and then down to the beach below the hut, where he makes another puzzling detour, this time to retrieve his canvas hat from the sea.

Only as they turn towards the hut does Romy herself emerge, her familiar fatigues drawn in at the waist with a belt, her hair pinned up under her desert hat. Removing her shades with her left hand she holds out the right in a ladylike way for the Emir to take, for all the world as if she had been expecting this very visit.

'You've timed it perfectly for breakfast, Your Highness,' she drawls.

Soon they are all gathered as equals on groundsheets eating creek fish and flat bread with their fingers. Tea stews over a fire of driftwood. The men from the barge have joined them, and Romy has explained to the Emir the outline of the submerged prehistoric harbour and how they are to lift with the pulley gear big hewn stones that formed the ancient quay.

A while later the Emir says, 'Your father has abandoned us to the *wolves*, Miss Romy.' He would collect English idioms like little artefacts of a distant culture.

She replies that that was not so at all. Her father thought of the Emir every day. Nowadays, the Emir could telephone him any time he wished.

'A Wazir in retirement in Gloss-erstershire,' the Emir objects, 'is not a Wazir. There are no wolves in Gloss-estershire.'

'There are no wolves here either,' Romy observes.

'Not here, but they are walking around.' The Emir makes a circling lope with a dangling fishbone.

'Jones is something of a wolf,' she adds.

The Emir frowns. 'You and Jonas should be married. I have said this before.' He has indeed. All women needed children. For years the Emir tried to marry her off to Richard Fenton, who courted her with etiolated hopelessness, first as her father's Second Secretary, then from his successive Middle Eastern postings.

'Jones is married already,' she says.

'You should become a Muslim, Jonas. I have said this before, also.'

Jones explains that he and his wife have agreed on desertion. It took three years, and there was one to go.

'Look how old is this Jonas already.'

'You'd be surprised,' says Romy.

The Emir turns to him. 'Then you will carry Miss Romy back to England. But we wish for you to stay, Jonas. You give the news for the *Morning Post* and the different papers. You can explain for me the policies of the world, Jonas. Amrika and Russia. The strings they are pulling. And you, Miss Romy: you make the history for the day before yesterday.'

Not long after, her father unexpectedly died. Already by then Jones had slipped into the role of confidant of the Emir. Romy flew to London for her father's memorial service in the crypt of St Paul's and while she was away from him she miscarried, very early, the baby they had not intended, though would have kept with joy. What was it telling them, that little loss of what they did not yet have?

The tide was going out now and it would soon be difficult even for a shallow-draughted *boum* to ride the bar at the mouth of the creek. He felt in his shirt pocket for the scrap of paper bearing the Emir's handwriting: it was not there. In the darkness he peered at the sand beside him, then scanned the space round about with his lighter. He found McCulloch's note. He opened the pages of his passport in case it was caught between them.

He searched his three trouser pockets. He wondered whether it might have slipped out when he was letting the air out of his tyres. He felt sure he had put it in his shirt not his trousers: he hadn't wanted to put it in his back pocket with the wallet in case he sat on it.

He hadn't the strength to go back for it, he knew that.

He questioned himself narrowly as to whether he cared what happened to the island. The politics of mankind would go its way irrespective of this or that. As for the Emir himself, indeed Jones cared for him; but did the old man truly wish to be restored to power? Now that all this had taken place, his shoulder ripped, and his days anyway few, wouldn't he now rather join his old friend Jonas in obliteration? Wouldn't that now be the counsel Jones would privately vouchsafe him – to be done with the world and secure as tranquil a passing as the caprice of it all would allow?

Now that he had lost the paper, he would sleep. It was the same now, whether the boat came or not. There was no purpose in his being here – no purpose in his being anywhere. In the past he supposed life had a purpose, some supreme justice to which the pain and waste were obscure but essential contributors. He now saw that the secret of life was that it had no secret. Perceiving this paradox was what he had over Hatim and Al-Bakr, and those smart-alec journalists in the Darwish.

Did they suppose they could dismiss him, the whipper-snappers, run rings round him? But he had out-compassed them all, he was gone already, self-diffused, nothing left of the past, nothing to come.

Lying here in the dark he recognised all of life to be bits brought fortuitously together, perhaps attaining momentary coherence, and falling away. Shaping and vanishing. Lives weren't grand opera justified by the whole cast in a *tutti fortissimo* finale. It was the same whether one had a state funeral or drifted away unnoticed against an abandoned cable drum.

Already he could hardly remember what might have so possessed him as to have brought him to this spot.

When he was a boy in Shropshire, the family's bull-terrier caught an old fox, brought it right into the front hall: it died there, on the flooring by the raincoats and shooting-sticks, its mouth stretching as it fought for breath for its pierced lung. Jones had thrown the body out into the woods behind the azaleas, wondering if he ought to have buried it. A few days later – oh, only three or four days – he had come across the carcase and already it was all but gone, a smudge of sandy fur among the weeds. Here the sand and the crabs and the light waves at high tide would take one in just as swiftly.

The sea's noise had retreated. He could hear fine music which he knew came from his head.

He slept crookedly against the cable drum with his bottle of water as a pillow until the sun was well up, then awoke and looked out on the entrance to the open sea. There was no *boum*, no boat of any kind. It was already 7 a.m. and with each minute of growing daylight the likelihood of the boat's putting in diminished. They would leave him here to die in peace. He wanted to go on sleeping; only his thirst stopped him, and all the water had escaped from the bottle while he slept because the thread was gone on the stopper. Moreover, flies had come with the rising heat – it was they that had woken him, guzzling the lacerations of his ankles, reopening the wounds with their fangs. He struggled dizzily to his feet and several crabs skeltered for the waves. He could ask for water at the huts five hundred yards up the creek. Then he could lie down again. He felt so faint and uncertain of himself.

A derelict earth structure, once whitewashed, stood back from the beach half-way to the fishermen's huts. It was a tiny mosque, now abandoned, which had been in occasional use at the time of Romy's excavations, and this was as far as Jones could drag himself along the cruel glaring beach. He pushed open the palm-wood door. The roof of russet mangrove poles and palm thatch was still mostly intact. A complex woven fish-trap occupied one end. Jones settled into the *qibla* niche recessed into the eastern wall. A skirmish of flies had followed him and began to feed on his sores again. He tried to cover the sores with little piles of sand, but the sand was so fine it flowed off his ankles and not enough stuck to the moist abrasions to pack them in. On a ledge beside the *qibla* lay a few dusty sheets of a Koran, once upon a time devoutly handwritten, which he folded round his ankles and tucked into the tops of his canvas shoes to keep them in place. Propped into the *qibla* again he fell into a confused sleep, wondering how long a holy place held its holiness after it was abandoned. He would prefer to die in a sanctified place. But for two or three blades of vicious sunlight, the roof still contained the shade: it was the sun, surely, that burned out the good djinns. Only a little new sand had leaked in through cracks in the walls and under the door.

As to the face of God – face or no face – he wasn't fussy. The Emir chose to take him as a species of Christian and had accommodated Jones's infidelism by describing him 'a man of the Book', although the only Christian church the devout old Muslim had permitted on his island was in the compound of the American Embassy. It was built in inter-denominational concrete with deal chairs and vibro organ and a terrible lack of mystery. Jones would rather die here with the local deity and the flies, at Romy's last place.

6

Romy, so experienced a skin-diver. It is Romy who has taught Jones.

It is afternoon, right here, in high summer, after the midday break, in blazing sun. Jones comes out from the shade of the palm-thatched hut. He is alone on the beach, with his canvas hat on, the sand too hot for his feet. He can hear his name being called from the barge by the Arab winchman, no urgency in the summons, the voice apologetic at disturbing his peace. He saunters down the beach, and cups his hand behind an ear to catch what the winchman is saying. Man and barge are only twenty-five yards from the water's edge where the wavelets lap.

'Excusey-me . . . our lady, may be she is too much *down*.'

The fellow taps his big wristwatch and grins. Jones focuses on him. He can see the winch drawing up a slack hawzer and a moment later the net breaks surface – a great rent in it. The winchman grins again sheepishly.

Jones knows at once. Under the burning sun his entire universe – horizon to horizon – shrivels to nothing. He blunders into the shallow waters, dives without equipment, is hauled back on board the barge, struggles into his diving gear blind with despair, goes down again. The other Arab crewmen lazily awake from their siesta.

Later he is squatting on the edge of the dunes, the overhang above the beach. The three crewmen are carrying Romy's body past the cable drum up the beach. Slowly, with ridiculous care. Jones is not looking directly at that tiny cortège, but towards the waves breaking and breathing. He knows how she is, her body still sealed in the black skin of the diving-suit and her head free and fair for death.

In those few minutes he has become an old man.

*

He lay as if he had been flung down. A grizzled and leathery gnome of a man and an ageless Moor, ugly and of great strength, were bending over the prone form. The gnome put out a brown hand to touch him.

'Misterr Jonas.'

The inert body did not respond. The newcomers could see he had urinated in his trousers. Suddenly the body was gripped by a convulsive inner force. A mumbled cry escaped him, 'Ro –!' and the newcomers recoiled.

'Misterr Jonas?'

Jones woke in alarm, crying 'Oh . . . oh!' He tried at once to stand, propped against the mosque wall, pulling his hat on, but he toppled sideways. His hat fell off.

The grizzled gnome said, 'Come,' which was one of his dozen words of English. The other man, a muscular black Moor, raised the Englishman to his feet so that he was leaning on him, and thus drew him out of the little mosque. All Jones's weight was supported by this Moor; and as the three of them moved down the beach towards a dory drawn up on the sand, the grizzled gnome, who was carrying Jones's radio and hat, picked up two leaves torn from a Koran which the long body of the Englishman seemed to have shed. After a few yards the Moor, though a good foot shorter than Jones, picked him up and carried him like a baby. Men and children emerged from the palm-frond huts up the creek to watch, a wise distance from strange events.

They manhandled Jones from the dory aboard the *boum* riding at anchor beyond the fish-traps. They could not make out whether or not he was aware of what was taking place. At times he spoke quite clearly, pushing them aside, gruffly establishing his right to master his own actions. Yet if they let him go he fell or floundered. They propped him up in shadow below, on a palliasse.

That some part of his body had ceased to function properly, he himself could have said. His low rage at the discontinuation of control was a low rage directed at himself, in that, by greater effort or circumspection he presumed he could have died completely, not just in some function. He had approached the house of death not by the front entrance but by a side-door and had entered only to find that the net of corridors gave no access to the main building. So he must find his way out again and re-enter by the front door. He could not achieve this by conscious but only by unconscious effort. These men had intruded upon his effort.

In the rolling darkness below deck he could resume the effort, but began to be troubled by fine music. He could have been borne away by this fine music as on King Arthur's barque but there was a distraction pulling against tranquil abandonment. It was a work for full choir and organ he had sung as a boy, the *Messiah* of Handel: it seemed a wonder that so small a boat could accommodate so vast a chorus and so mighty an organ. What snagged the marvel was that his solo part was approaching. Of course he knew the music, had known it all his life. Yet he hadn't rehearsed it for years and wasn't sure when he was to come in: he had not got his score, and chorus and organist were oblivious of this as they swept on. Moreover he was unkempt and dirty and in his anxiety at his solo he had passed water in his trousers which he could smell as well as the musk of *qatt* on the palliasse.

When he opened an eye he could see the swarthy crewman squatting beside him with a platter of dates and a drink he knew to be goat's milk with honey. The man chewed *qatt* as he waited to feed him. As soon as Jones raised his head, this black man put the tumbler of sweetened milk to his lips. Jones sipped and choked, and resumed sipping, taking the glass from the black hand. The rhythm of the organ had become the beat of the engine. There was no music now, only the stinging wetness of his own urine down his trouser leg.

He munched slowly through half the plate of dates. Shrunk and bowed, the gnomish skipper descended, like one coming home to his hole in the tree-roots. He smiled congratulation at his passenger's appetite. Jones asked him his name and he replied it was Nasir. He asked where they were going and Captain Nasir replied with the name of the mainland port.

Then he remembered what was expected of him, and that he had lost the Emir's paper. He looked at the captain with distraught eyes and shook his head. It was a pointless voyage, dangerous and pointless. Nasir leaned forward and placed his hand on the Inglisi's shoulder, but Jones's eyes were filling with tears. He repeated to the captain several times that he had lost the Emir's paper, but the Arab could not understand and thought the stroke had made him maudlin.

Jones burst out at him, 'It's no good my filing without the bloody paper,' and Nasir withdrew his hand.

'Bluddi-paipr,' Nasir parroted regretfully.

Jones put his fingers into his shirt pocket and immediately found the Emir's paper. He drew it out very carefully and looked at it with dull humour. It was as if someone had taken it and returned it: he watched himself as he ceased to wish to die.

A distance away men have come to his doorway – two soldiers stepping down from a military jeep. First they knock, then they bang, on the strong door of his old house. Now one starts prising at the lock with a bayonet. The door gives.

They swagger-run down the dark passage as if he could be dangerous to them or make a dash for safety. They thrust open each of the doors – the bedroom, the bathroom, his malodorous kitchen. In the *majlis* they yank open all the drawers. On the worn rug they make a great heap of all the papers they can find – old dispatches, cuttings, letters, photographs. They lift off from his desk the column of typescript and the labour of notes in their alien script and dump it all on top of the jumbled heap. They roll up this great mess of writing in the rug and begin to carry it out. One of them spots the letter against the amphora: he puts it in his pocket.

As they pass through the patio with their burden, the parrot watches them from its cage. The first soldier flicks open the door of the cage and the second soldier mocks it with a squawk.

Jones pushed the fragment of paper towards Captain Nasir. The muscular black man popped another date into his mouth as if he were a baby.

The wizened skipper took the paper and laid it reverently

beside him. He pulled out a bundle from against the ribs of the vessel by the tool-box and unwound it slowly. He took out a pair of spectacles which he fitted in an exact manner on to his nose. Then he stood so that the light from the hatch fell on the tiny paper, the movement of his lips telling the pace of his reading. He read it twice, and in the course of the second reading his head began to nod with a slow vigour. When he had finished he passed the paper back to Jones with both hands like the most destructible of palimpsests, shut his spectacles, ceremoniously wound them up in the old head-cloth and replaced them in their corner against the ship's ribs. Then he put out his hard, narrow hand and took Jones's right hand, swollen with prickly heat, and lightly held it for several seconds. When his hand was released, Jones raised his fingers to his lips. Even now, news of the paper in his possession reaching the wrong ears on the quayside might cheat his poor heart of the privilege of ending him.

He fumbled for his Kensitas and they lit one for him. He peered at his watch. In London it was already 9 a.m. He indicated his wish to go up on deck, and they helped him up the ladder he had no recollection of descending. His left leg had forgotten its function and had lost respect for his will. They brought him a box to sit on under the sailcloth awning. He scanned the horizon. They were steaming south for the mainland, not yet half-way across the straits. Both mainland and the island were visible in the midday haze, each a low dun smudge. Two oil tankers were steaming east, down-Gulf, through this same strait; no other vessels were visible except a small flotilla of fishing boats far ahead between their own *boum* and the mainland. No one appeared to be in pursuit. It was a paradigm of tranquillity. High sun and shallow waters were in league to blotch and dapple the constant, exquisite changeability. Over the throb of engine a high melisma wove from the throat of the young helmsman. At six or seven knots the drift of air lifted away oppression of heat. Yet how exposed they were, isolated on this ocean, their route as plain as a confession. And now with following thunder three aircraft from the island's fighter wing streaked out above them, spanning their strait in seconds, seeing all.

The black Moor brought him a faded loincoth, and took away his trousers.

He struggled to hold fast to what he knew he must do. At two o'clock he picked up the BBC news: 11 a.m. London time: in the *Post*'s newsroom the department heads would be assembling in the Editor's office for the morning conference. The bulletin carried nothing new on the night before except that a dozen more states had recognised the island's new regime, including two Western powers, namely Canada and Sweden – thus currying (he perceived) a smidgeon of popularity with the Reds and Third World riff-raff in the UN with typical timely cant. He supposed the report by the Reuters man had had its influence; and once again his stomach tightened at the thought that even now in conference they were provisionally slotting his own 'interview' with the Emir, for want of anything better, despite its bizarre annulment. For they always liked to have their own man's byline up there on top of a column of print when the news was big. And surely, too, the foreign desk would already have been pleading for contact with him by the only line of communication – the palace telex – open to them ... Meanwhile that Reuters weasel (so quiet, so smug) would be allowed to get away another dispatch today, further confirming the *coup* as an act of popular revolution. It was the familiar sorry sequence.

He pictured those upstart journalists at the Darwish, each with his own little plan for moving his copy, each one's report with its own embellishments and angles on the central half-truths fed them by the usurpers. He knew that Fuad Al-Bakr would permit no other reporter to see the Emir – and most certainly not now that they would have awoken to his deception ... They would be looking for him now, and finding him gone, order a search. Maybe it was providential the old Packard had got stuck. But it pointed to the creek, and the fisherman there would have seen him, and the *boum*. No one can hide in empty land. Then they could either send a patrol boat in pursuit, or have people waiting for him at the mainland port on the off chance.

He pulled himself to his feet. All three Arabs aboard – Nasir, the Moor, and the helmsman – watched him, and under all their eyes he dragged himself aft along the rail to the thunderbox that hung over the stern on the starboard side. Having done his number one in his trousers, he was not going to disgrace himself with number two. The thunderbox had a little door like a pulpit – from the seaward side it actually resembled a pulpit, being quite finely carved and painted. He squatted there, so tall, shoulders and head sticking out above like a legless preacher ranting at the sea. He squatted on under the flailing sun and when he was done he found he could not drag himself upright. He called weakly to the helmsman who summoned the Moor for'ard from where he had been washing his trousers in a bucket. Draped over them, he was helped by the two men back to his box under the awning while the skipper moved to the tiller.

He leaned back exhausted. How could he go on with this? His mind was good but his body half-gone. The Moor brought water, soap, a cloth, and half a razorblade held in a stick; he shaved him with extreme care. He declared his name repeatedly, *Ismail*, and assured Jones he was his servant. Jones could see what an ugly fellow he was and also how gentle and strong. He took out Jones's Kensitas and lit one cigarette for Jones and one for himself. A little later he returned with an empty dark red Rothman's box. He made Jones put the Emir's paper in the Rothman's box.

Jones found his spectacles and began to draft his dispatch on the back of McCulloch's letter. He wrote with difficulty because of his long sight and because there was nothing on which to rest the paper except the up-turned base of the plastic bucket. He gave the island as his dateline, and began:

'The legitimacy of the new government claiming power here since early yesterday has been categorically repudiated by the Emir himself, Ahmed al-Asnan, in a statement handwritten and signed by himself and passed by him to me as correspondent of the *Morning Post*.

'The statement specifically refutes the announcement of the "voluntary" abdication disseminated by his son, Hatim, and Fuad Al-Bakr in support of their claim to power.'

He used Hatim's gold pen, and, as he wrote, black Ismail on his haunches close beside watched with lips made loose by wonder.

'Misterr.'

Jones looked at the Moor over his glasses. The man gave him a slow grin and spread his arms, making a scanning swing with his head, like someone reading an open newspaper.

Jones grinned too. 'Right, Ismail, right!'

He resumed writing, quoting the text of the Emir's paper in English translation, and then relating exactly how it reached him. Any such exposure of facts jeopardised the old man's safety: that he recognised. Yet a public announcement was what the Emir must have wanted, and the details that authenticated the handwritten message were essential. He knew well just what impact this exclusive would have internationally; the cold sweat in the palms of his hands told him the urgency of it. He would make it clean and strong and factual. If the whipper-snappers in the Darwish had the story they would editorialise in the very first paragraph – *In a move that will further heighten Middle East instability, the Emir Ahmed al-Asnan has today released a message openly defying . . .'* and so on, brazenly mushing up the facts with comment of their own. When he was in Fleet Street, if you wanted to include comment on an event you bloody well had to find someone to make it and then quote him, or the subs would have it out.

He kept glancing at his watch. He and the old hulk were as one, straining through the water at a handful of knots. He saw his trousers drying on the deck. The sun already leaned to the west. He felt in himself the throb and purpose of the diesel, yet still could not quite gather himself; fragments were unresolved, pieces of his past life, like tendrils of weed reaching up from the opaline seabed. Their own sunlight freely entered and illuminated this marine territory, making perpetual play of opalescence, and it was all so close beneath them, so very close that they must sometimes throttle back to two or three knots to navigate over it safely. Moreover, it was exquisitely beautiful. Yet however close, it was of a quite different order from their own airy, surface order: and those who belonged to it like

Romy could not be reached even though their tendrils floated upwards as if to clutch at them.

They throbbed and pushed on across this sea-veil cast down immemorially between the island he had escaped from and the greater land he must at all costs gain, until at last one smudge had all but dissolved into the horizon and the smudge ahead grew strong and sharp and filled their eyes.

As this new land drew them in, they curved through a small flotilla of fishing boats and were an object of curiosity. Ismail brought him his laundered trousers which were stiff and dry.

In the distant Darwish, Lou Rivers, agitated, is searching for someone in the lobby. Rivers has been agitated for fully one and a half days, but his agitation at this moment has a quality of special urgency. He has in his hand a single sheet of paper. Soldiers still guard the hotel entrance, and every guest that wishes to leave the premises must show his documents and write down where he intends to go, and why, and when he intends to return.

Rivers hurries into the atrium. There he encounters Carew of Reuters, evidently his quarry, briskly leaving the bar-room.

'Hey, Shaun. I was looking for you. Just look at this.'

He hands him the piece of paper. It is a photostat of a brief and tightly penned piece of Arabic handwriting and a crude English translation, in handwritten capitals, appended beneath.

Carew shoots his fellow journalist a glance of weasel wariness. He hands back the paper. 'It's not going to help any of us, that message,' he says. 'Trying to send that out won't assist us at all.'

Rivers is affronted. 'It's central to the story,' he declares. 'It discredits the *coup*.'

'It'll be the last time they let you back on the island.'

'If they hang on to it,' Rivers ripostes with a snuff. He has met this before, news agency men putting it across television reporters, making them look like amateurs at gathering news.

'I thought you fancied the rebels,' Carew says.

'It's not my job to fancy anybody,' Rivers informs him. He's not going to have a Reuters man teaching him his business. Ever since the *coup* occurred, Carew had been scurrying about with a knowing look on his face.

'Look, chum,' Carew says. 'It's not even authenticated, that Arabic. Anybody could have written it.'

'That's the first step, obviously,' Rivers says, reasserting his professionalism. 'Authenticate. McCulloch could do that.'

'You're on your own, chum.'

Rivers admits he doesn't know how to find McCulloch. His newspaper is shut down: he lives somewhere in the town, and his telephone is cut off.

Carew gives him one of his knowing looks. 'Tough shit,' he says, and hurries on.

They tied up at the mainland port's small boats' quay at a quarter to one London time. It was still high afternoon locally and a good period to handle officials: at that hour most were absent and the sleepy remnant had no wish to prolong their duties. Jones came ashore leaning on Ismail, left leg dragging. It was rare enough for a European to come in by *boum*, but the immigration officer at a desk littered with red Vimto cans seemed to accept the validity of Jones's multiple visa and health documents without a quaver.

Jones limped out of the shed into the glare, flanked by the gnomish shipmaster Nasir and the swarthy Ismail. An incongruous trio. Two yellow Datsun taxis stood against the wall of the customs building opposite, trying to snuggle in under the bar of the shade. One taxi already contained a driver and two passengers. The driver of the other was asleep under the covered entrance to the building, and Nasir crossed to wake him. Jones was eased into the cramped vehicle and Ismail rode beside him in the back. Jones told the driver to take them to the office of the local newspaper, which he named. At the port area barrier a guard emerged from his box to inspect the car. He spotted the Rothman's packet in the Englishman's shirt pocket and motioned that he required a cigarette. Jones offered him his Kensitas; but the man said 'Rothman's' and lifted out the packet deftly with two fingers. Finding it empty of cigarettes he tossed it aside on to the macadam. Nasir ordered Ismail to fetch it, and as he was doing so Jones noticed the other taxi drawing up behind.

The two taxis went through the barrier in convoy. Jones could see the other taxi behind in the mirror. He changed his instructions and told the driver to take them to the oil company's regional headquarters. He had not been at this game for fifty-odd years for nothing. The oil company buildings were enclosed in a compound ringed by high mesh-fences: nobody could follow them in there.

At the main gate barrier they were obliged to get out of their taxi. It was harder getting out than in: Jones as near as anything toppled: only the great strength of Ismail prevented it. The American guard had come out of the gatehouse, a thick sallow man, armed.

Nothing was going to be easy. It was the sheer primitiveness of his companions that made them so out of place here – dark, weathered men in sun-bleached loincloths, and their feet, though sandalled now, manifestly accustomed to nakedness.

Across the wide approach, the other taxi had pulled up: no one got out.

'Someone expecting ya?' the guard said.

Jones told him who, lying.

'Doubtful he'll be in right now,' the guard said, not budging. 'Everyone gone for the day.' It was as good as a prohibition. He was a slow man, with feet apart.

'He's expecting me,' Jones assured him, with his every grace, very English. 'Don't worry – we have a fixed date.' He looked at his watch. 'Five o'clock.' He was thankful Ismail had shaved him. A harmless old man.

'Okay bud, I'll ring through.'

'Don't trouble yourself. Just let me sign the visitor's sheet, if you'd be kind enough.'

'Lemme ring through.' There was an adopted assertiveness about the man's speech, a caricature American-ness that told Jones his childhood language had not been English but, perhaps, Spanish. He turned towards the gatehouse and Jones indicated to his companions at once that they should follow. An Arab guard, also in company uniform, looked up, puzzled.

Jones got himself right up beside the American guard's telephone. There on the desk, sure enough, stood a nameplate of rusticised varnished wood and the name engraved in fancy script and touched up with gold paint, *Jim Garcia*. The man had the printed directory of company employees in his hand.

'Who ya wanna see, then, mister?'

'Gerry Norbert,' Jones said. 'Public Affairs.' He had his glasses on now. 'If you'd just remind me of his number, Jim.' The man was almost certainly baptised Jaime, and his translation to Jim the most important step in his life. 'Isn't it four something? . . .' Jones had his hand on the telephone and was looking down on the man amiably.

'N-o-r-?'

'Exactly,' Jones congratulated. 'Norbert.'

'Thirty-seven forty-two.'

'*Three*, of course.' It was Jones who raised the telephone. 'Three-seven-four-two,' he repeated as he dialled. He held the receiver tight against his ear, and let it ring twice before he spoke. 'Gerry? It's Gran Jones here.' Pause. 'Hi. I'm right here at the gate. Your efficient gate guard and I wanted to check you'd stayed in for me.' Pause. 'I'll be right up. Cheers.'

He put the receiver back and smiled at the guard. No one had answered.

'May I sign your visitors' log?'

The guard scarcely had an option, without risk of losing face. He passed across the clipboard. 'You're okay. Your friends'll haveta wait.'

Jones took his time filling in his entry. He could smell Nasir and Ismail – the good odour of the skin of men who labour in sea air. As he wrote he echoed aloud the pen's movement – name, time in, company represented, whom he was visiting. Give people time, the old old trick. Only after he had signed did he raise his eyes. 'What was that you said, Jim?'

'Your friends'll haveta wait.'

But he knew the 'Jim' was like a brushing kiss.

'I've got to have them.' His face was full of apology for age and infirmity, from which none was exempt. 'I've only one leg that works. I've really got to have them.'

'Wassa trouble?'

'A little paralysis.'

'You want the sanatorium, buddy.'

Jones grinned a sort of dismissive assent, which said, But what could anyone do for me now? The thought of medical treatment hadn't once entered his head throughout their voyage from the island.

'Okay, granpa. Sign 'em up. No, they must sign. Who are they anyway? Can they write?' The guard summoned his Arab counterpart. 'They each gotta give the names.'

'For God's sake, Jim,' Jones said mildly.

He was a master when it came to barriers. When all was done and he was limping between his companions to the main administration building which housed the communications centre he felt that same glow in the soul of any man who has put mastery to use. But the sun was still fierce and a dizziness bothered him like a swarm of gnats.

He directed his trio straight along the principal ground floor corridor towards the telex room. Nobody was about. A light shone through the frosted glass of the telex room. All three newcomers pushed in together: a young American unknown to Jones was on late telex duty in charge of a console of four machines, one of which was in action.

'My name is Jones,' he opened in his courtly manner. 'This is Captain Nasir and this is Mr Ismail. I am correspondent of the London *Post* and I have to telex an urgent dispatch.'

The young man smiled emptily, shook each hand as it was put out, but kept his own name to himself. The presence of Arabs made him diffident. He was poorly built and his head seemed too heavy for his body. It took him a while to grasp Jones's intention, and Jones omitted to explain the reason for his escort. He said in a flat voice: 'You'll need your message cleared by Public Affairs, sir. They'll be in at 8 a.m. tomorrow.'

'I am a friend of Mr Burroughs, your President,' Jones told him assuringly.

'Mr Burroughs is in Washington.'

'I know.'

Of course he knew: once he got in among the local officials of the company, they'd huff and puff, especially when they found it to be news of obvious international importance. They'd crosscheck and doublecheck and finally pass the buck to headquarters in Washington.

'So you'll have to clear it with Public Affairs tomorrow. I'm sorry.'

'Don't be sorry,' Jones said quietly. Nothing was going to be easy. 'Tomorrow's too late. Look, I'll show you the dispatch.'

When Jones moved, the Arabs moved with him like a bizarre drill-routine. They sat him at the machine next to the one in operation. World commodity prices were coming in.

'Everyone goes home at two, here. Eight to two, that's it.'

'You don't have a wirephoto facility?' Jones asked.

'No, we don't. And you can't use this telex, either.' The diffidence had gone: it was hot sulk now.

'I'm just going to show you the dispatch,' Jones purred. 'I'm not transmitting, dear boy.'

Jones, pressed the PREP key and began at once to type. As he tapped, his message came up on the screen.

'Listen, sir' – the young man's voice rising – 'we only allow qualified operators.'

'I know. I am qualified. I'm seventy-six years old. I am qualified.' Jones did not even turn to talk to him.

'Not here,' the young man returned, and crossed to hit the CLEAR button. The message on the screen vanished.

Jones folded his arms. He sat there large and uncoordinated and tired beyond resting. He was impervious to any hostility. He put out a hand and touched PREP: the light came on again and the machine was in readiness. The young man hit CLEAR again.

Ismail stepped up and stood right beside the young man. He lightly laid his black hand on his arm. Jones hit PREP again and resumed typing. The American did not move. What he wrote was:

'FLASH. JONES HERE. I HAVE LEFT ISLAND WITH EXCLUSIVE EVIDENCE SIGNED BY THE EMIR PROVING NEW REGIME IS NOT

REPEAT NOT LEGITIMATE. THIS EVIDENCE I SHALL WIREPHOTO FROM LOCAL NEWSPAPER HERE. MEANWHILE STANDBY MY DISPATCH AND INFORM EDITOR. ARE U READY?'

He stopped.

'Okay, that's enough,' the young man said.

None of them paid him noticeable attention. Jones's great blotched hands were poised over the machine. He typed the *Post*'s number.

The answerback came up instantly. It was always a good moment, like a password exchanged across half the world. It was still early afternoon in London, but most of them should be back from lunch. Jones hit the SEND button. As his 'flash' message was printing out on the paper roller, he propped up his handwritten draft under the paper arm on the front of the machine: it wasn't easy to decipher.

He flicked to open-line transmission and typed: 'ANYONE THERE?'

'YES,' came the answer. 'MOM.' Then, 'OK FILE AWAY.' Jones typed his dateline and time slug and started: 'THE LEGITIMACY OF THE NEW GOVERNMENT CLAIMING −'

'OK, you win,' the duty man broke out. 'You hold it, I'll call the people from Public Affairs out from home. They'll pass your message.'

'Too late, I fear,' Jones replied.

The young man reached forward quickly and hit CLEAR.

'Fuck you,' Jones said. 'You've broken the contact. Ismail,' he continued in Arabic, 'hold him.'

The instantaneousness of the response to the command took even Jones by surprise: Ismail swung the young man round, gripped his shoulders, butted him in the face, flung him to the floor, and stood on his neck with one broad sandalled foot, while simultaneously pulling upwards and twisting an arm, and grinning seraphically. A low whimper trickled out of the young man like an oozing of blood and mucus.

'I'm bound to tell you, dear boy,' Jones addressed him through the whimper, 'that if it became essential to kill you, I would have it done with pleasure.'

After he got the *Post* wireroom again he found them upset, but this time moved the whole dispatch, though he mis-keyed frequently and had to restart several lines since the fingers of one hand proved not obedient. When he came to the dangerous passage about how the Emir passed him the message he did not pause or waver, for this was their common risk: the transmission and exposition of this story was what, if need be, the Emir would give his last breath for, as he, Jones, would also: two old blood-brothered men each in his given function.

When he had moved the complete dispatch he was spent and trembling. Nothing came back. He hit the BELL key. London wrote 'MOM'.

A further pause. Then, 'CHIEF SUB HERE. YOU THERE GRAN?' 'WHAT ELSE?' Cunt.

'HOW COME YESTERDAY U FILED MESSAGE ENDING BUST BUST AND NO FURTHER EXPLANATION?'

'WAS FORCED TO FILE IT BY EMIRS SON HATIM.'

'U REALLY THREW US HERE.'

'TANT PIS. TWAS YOUR DAY OFF.'

'U CANT DO THAT TO US, GRAN.'

'COME HERE AND DO BETTER.'

A silence ensued. Jones was glowering at the machine, at a lifetime of newsroom crassness.

'DID U QUERY MY BUST TELEX?'

'YES BUT NO JOY. THEY SAID THEY WOULD FIND U.'

'I TOLD U NOT TO CALL BACK.'

'WE HAD TO TRY.'

'U MIGHT HAVE KILLED ME.'

'WE SENT U 3 WIRES TO DARWISH.'

The Darwish! A jam-jar of bluebottles.

'DARWISH SEALED OFF. CABLE OFFICE SHUT ANYWAY.'

'REUTERS MANAGED TO FILE FROM ISLAND.'

'BUT NOT THE FACTS.' The bastard. 'HAVE U READ WHAT I JUST SENT?'

'MOM.'

Foreign subs, to a man, were dolts, dyed in the wool, to whom abroad meant package tours to the Costa Brava. This one was possessed of the infuriating propensity to write headlines that slightly distorted the copy. Jones had met him on his last visit to London. He wouldn't have known where to look for the island in his school atlas.

'FINISHED?' Jones typed.

'MOM. TIS NOT CLEAN COPY.'

'LISTEN, I WANT EDITOR READ THIS STORY BEFORE I SWITCH OFF.' His hands were shaking fearfully; how they still functioned for him he knew not. All that drove him now was a pure pulsing anger.

'WE CALL U BACK.'

'WONT BE HERE. HAVE COMMANDEERED THIS TELEX AND MY FRIEND IS HOLDING DOWN OPERATOR BY STANDING ON NECK.'

'MOM.'

What did the dolt suppose it was like? Sending in cricket scores from the press-box at Lords?

'MOM,' again.

Then the Foreign Editor came on.

'FOSTER HERE. TREMENDOUS STORY, GRAN. CONGRATS. COULD BE PAGE ONE LEAD IF U CAN WIREPHOTO EMIR'S ACTUAL HANDWRITTEN MESSAGE.'

'WILL TRY PRONTO. NO FACILITIES HERE.' Foster knew the field, once a foreign reporter himself: half his age, naturally, but knew the field a bit. Foster could spot the big story when it was put under his nose ... What the hell did he mean *Could be*? They were always covering their backsides, the dodgy executives.

'WHEN CAN WE EXPECT, GRAN?'

'ONE HOUR. MAYBE 2.'

'NOT LONGER THAN 2 IF POSS.'

Foster at least had a feel for the hot world at crisis time. Jones could have told him he had a stroke last night.

'WE THINK AUTHENTICATION ESSENTIAL,' the machine said.

'NATCH.'

'YDAY U HAD US AT 6S AND 7S.'

'TWAS DIFFERENT THEN.'

'UNDERSTOOD. WHERE WILL U BE LATER?'

Later? What later? 'WILL TELL U WHEN I WIREPHOTO.'

'OK. TKS. BI.'

He could feel them pulling away, wanting him to let go of them.

'IF EDITOR WANTS TO PHONE DOWNING STREET WITH MAIN SUBSTANCE, MAKE SURE NO LEAKS TO OPPOSITION.' By which he meant the other dailies.

'DONT WORRY. BI.'

'TWILL PUT CAT AMONG PIGEONS.'

'SOME PIGEONS. CONGRATS & BI.'

'OK BIBI.'

The machine's chatter ceased and London cleared with a kind of sigh. Jones ripped the top copy off the paper roller. The young American had given up whimpering. Ismail looked at Jones enquiringly. He signalled to let him up.

Ismail held him by the wrist as he got awkwardly to his feet. One ear was a deep red and a discoloration spread across the neck where Ismail's broad foot had rested.

Jones opened his wallet.

'Please accept my card. Send me the bill for the telex call. A copy of my dispatch is on your machine. We are not to have the pleasure of killing you. But if you dare make any move to prevent me or my friends leaving this compound, I will tell the world through my newspaper that this company supported the Marxist leaders of the *coup d'état* on the island by attempting to suppress the truth. Are you clear?' His speech was wonderfully unimpaired.

The young man's eyes brimmed but no words came.

Now little Nasir and Ismail helped Jones to his feet. As they left the room in their strange trio drill-routine the young man was sitting on a swivel chair, face in hands.

Jones was elated. Two congrats: Foster had grasped the significance of the story all right – the repudiation of legitimacy, the role of the foreign 'training unit'. It could yet be in time to forestall big power recognition, and raise the spectre of intervention. Foster was a good bloke, despite that *Could be*. 'Some pigeons'! – but did Foster not see he was referring to Fleet Street rivals, not the usurpers?

It was nearly dark, the sun gone, prayer finished. The featureless landscape, dissolved into various deep colours, had regained its secrets and was pricked with lights. Half-night had replaced the plumes of smoke by vivid orange torches of the last remaining gas flare-offs, and the scent of a hidden industry lay across mile on mile of desert.

Exhilaration and his escort carried Jones all the way to the main gate. The pipsqueaks in the Darwish – how he would like to witness their faces when they got the playback from London. And now he wondered if Paul would see tomorrow's *Post*. He gave a chuckle.

Ismail answered him, chuckle for chuckle.

Jones said, 'Maybe my grandchildren will see the paper tomorrow.'

'Anjilden,' Ismail echoed.

'Tomorrow,' Nasir repeated sagely, being a word he recognised.

The gate guard merely nodded them through without leaving his box. The other taxi seemed to have vanished, but their own was still waiting and Jones was bundled in as before, in the back with Nasir, Ismail in front, and all the windows open to ventilate.

They moved out of the built-up area that surrounded the oil company compound and the neighbouring College of Petroleum Technology. The broad illuminated highway took them in thin traffic across a stretch of open desert, past the turning back to the seaport and the slip-road to the airport. Jones felt in his pocket for the Rothman's pack: the Emir's message was safe. As a small boy at school on Wenlock Edge he and his fellows used to play 'The Baron's Game'. One of the masters was the captive Baron, with about a quarter of the boys assigned to guard him in his glade in the woodlands. The rest were each given a little slip of paper representing some personal possession like 'the Baron's gold watch' or 'the Baron's false teeth' that had to be smuggled through to him, evading his custodians. Though tall for his age, Jones was greatly celebrated for worming past the defenders and pulling off that last desperate dash with his vital object . . .

Another vehicle was unexpectedly pulling alongside them. The occupants were calling, gesticulating – young Arabs. What recklessness was this? As the two cars slowed for the lights, they were accosting him, Jones, with shouts and leering faces through the open window. 'Inglisi!' they yelled. 'Inglisi!' They looked like North Africans – Egyptians, Libyans. Their teeth were bared at him, snarling. What madmen these mainland drivers were! Their car swayed and swerved alongside, inches away. And now one of them was trying to pass Jones some object, some small thing held in the hand thrusting out of the window. The other taxi leapt to mind, the threat it portended, how he had been marked on landing.

'No!' Jones roared. He fumbled for his window winder. 'No! NO!' and recoiled, but the youth continued to thrust the object across, and they swerved away, laughing and waving, the object tumbling off the back of the front seat to the floor at Jones's feet, where he supposed it would kill them on the instant. At Jones's alarm, their driver had yanked the taxi to a halt at the roadside.

Not all that far away, which is to say, across the dark straits, at Jones's only home, Sandy McCulloch is knocking on the door, with Rivers beside him. He does not knock too hard, for although the alley is empty they are breaking curfew and could be shot. There is still a remnant of daylight in the street, enough for them to see the new red Arabic slogan scrawled on the white wall. McCulloch whispers, 'They may have taken him in. I couldn't get him yesterday either.'

'Poor old crock,' Rivers says.

They have come here because Jones is the one man McCulloch can trust to authenticate the Emir's handwriting on the photostats now secretly circulating in the town, all descendents of the copy covertly made from Jones's original by Suleiman's son. Their idea is that if it proved genuine, McCulloch should sneak into his newspaper offices and wirephoto it to Associated Press – the rival news agency to Reuters – of which McCulloch is the accredited stringer. Actually, this is Rivers's plot, since he is intensely frustrated at being prevented from reporting for television, and now wishes to embarrass the usurpers and engage in some journalistic daredevilry. 'Just to stir it up, you mean, Lou?' McCulloch has queried, but Rivers, to whom McCulloch defers on the grounds both of his fame and his own temporary recruitment as guide to 'The World This Week', assured him it was central to the story and would give the other side a 'shot in the arm'. 'But they're occupying our building,' McCulloch persisted. At which Rivers looked at him with disdain, adding that if nothing was ventured, nothing was fucked. Sandy McCulloch caught a whiff of sacrificial role-playing, yet Rivers has persuaded him as far as here.

McCulloch finds one half of the door to be unbolted. Indeed, it seems to have been forced. He pushes it open.

'Gran?' he calls quietly.

They enter by the dark passage. A light burns. The parrot's cage is open and the bird gone. They move to the *majlis*. The parrot watches them from foliage in the narrow strip of garden.

The *majlis* is in a shambles, all the drawers yanked out, tipped upside down, cushions scattered, books heaped on the floor. The place has been raped. Rivers is pained for the old man. 'Holy shit,' he says. 'He's had visitors.'

'Official,' McCulloch endorses.

'They taken him in?'

'His car isn't outside.'

They move back through the patio to the bedroom: it is in a similar state of violation.

'What now, Lou? No point in trying to send a thing like this unauthenticated.'

The voice from the garden freezes them.

'Bye-bye Trudi.'

With good foot first, then a shaking hand, Jones fumbled for the object on the taxi's floor and retrieved it – viprous, ludicrously tiny, sharp-edged. A light inconsequential box. He had to put on his spectacles to decipher the lettering by the streetlighting: a cassette tape of the Rolling Stones. What better to appeal to so manifestly English a man, far from home, than a taste of his traditional music – a gesture of spontaneous Arab generosity well worth a little virtuoso driving.

7

'The thing's on the blink more often than not,' Williams said with breezy desperation in his Taffy accent, frowning above the black sheen of his mechanic's head. Just at this moment he wanted beyond anything in the world to be of use to the old man. 'Half an hour ago you could have caught the B.A. flight with it. That's it now.'

Distant thunder of a jet after take-off was audible. Jones was lumped into a narrow basket chair across from the wirephoto machine like a discarded outer garment. Deadline for the first edition of the *Post* had come and gone. Jones had told London by telex of a 'technical hitch': London hadn't reacted – not a word. At least he hadn't had to underline his ultimate failure, shout it in their ears, that it was this machine or nothing. And so, now, nothing ... They'd change the second edition front page for any damn silly thing – they *liked* changing it – but in forty-five minutes they'd be screwing down the second edition. For the third or fourth printings, the big runs, nothing but massive news would persuade them to remake – a Royal death, a shock defeat of the Government. Something of that order.

The Indian mechanic Williams had dug out from his home was tinkering and dithering with a stagey urgency. The machine's parts were laid out on newspaper on the floor. There was no telling if he actually knew what he was doing, though the probability was that he didn't.

'There's another flight tomorrow,' Williams offered.

'For God's sake,' Jones retorted. Did Williams understand nothing? The flight just gone didn't get to Heathrow until 6 a.m. The story was worthless after tomorrow – that is, after tonight's London paper. Politically worthless, and journalistically worthless too. At best a footnote. What else did *accompli* mean in *fait accompli*? After tomorrow nothing reported internationally could help the Emir: he might be dead by then anyway – would *rather* be dead, surely, if only because the shits would rather he survived.

Jones too would have had him survive, his dear old blood-buddy – survive long enough to learn that he, Jones, meant not to fail him, hadn't dumped him as Suleiman's son and suchlike were ready to. He would have had the Emir just to *know*, just be touched by that ebbing glow of very ancient comradeship. Then they could rot together, wrapped in the same stinking blanket, loose yellowed skin over old bones. He would have wished just that, nothing more . . . nothing more except, aha!, the joy of seeing the superiority wiped off Hatim's little mouth and the smirks vanish, *wupp*, from the faces of the whipper-snappers in the Darwish when they read tomorrow's *Post*. The joy of it!

That wouldn't happen now.

He let Williams top up the tumbler of *siddiqi*-tonic on the corner of the desk beside him. Two or three empty bottles of tonic water stood guard there, another, half-empty, at his feet. Williams himself settled back behind one of the room's four desks, and the bottle of colourless sugar-spirit bobbed in mid-desk between them like a buoy on a woozy sea.

Was there not about failure, abject failure, Jesus-failure, a quality of *depth* that must always elude the triumphant? A truth lay there that nagged him lately.

He realised he had forgotten about his obit; and, more, he didn't care about it any longer.

Through half-opened eyes he saw the giblets of electronic gadgetry ranged on the newspaper and the Hindi fussing over them; and the vision of a shrunken little chef, quite daft, pre-paring a fiasco of a banquet which the guests had already quit in disgust, roused a smile that did not quite reach his lips.

This cramped, low-ceilinged room had for him a toytown familiarity. This Williams had attempted to parcel it off with notices hung from the ceiling – 'Domestic', 'Foreign', 'Sports' and 'Photo'. The plywood door leading off to Williams's very own cubicle had a frosted glass panel bearing the word Editor. Diagonally across the ceiling a much bigger notice was sus-pended, demanding ACCURACY FIRST LAST AND ALWAYS.

The mechanic worked away like the dotty cook under a strip light in the corner designated 'Photo'. The machine itself wasn't any bigger than the average typewriter, but its ingredients, spread out on sheets of Williams's newspaper, seemed to cover half the floor and some would crawl away if he didn't watch out and buck up.

It was too late now. As good as.

London hadn't the courage to confirm that they wouldn't run his report until they got the picture; they'd just gone mum. But he knew, he knew their little *apparatchik* minds. They would *set* his copy, *set* it, yes . . . and sit on it until they got corroboration. He could hear Back Bench calling across to Foreign Desk: '*Anything on agency yet, Jack?*'/'Wha'? That ex-Emir?'/'*Tha'srigh*'. *Ahmed A-Wotsit.*'/'Not a dicky bird.'/'*No sign of Gran's little message from Pictures, either.*'/'He's over the hill, poor old Gran.' There was always the chance of an old reporter fabricating, a die-hard sucking a wrinkled thumb.

'*Die-hard,*' Jones muttered.

Williams glanced up. Surely he heard something. 'What d'you say, Gran?'

'Nothing.'

But Jones *had* said something. Was it *Tired*? An odd comment, just like that. Williams couldn't make him out. For example, was Jones looking at him? Ever since he had arrived the old man's eyes seemed to have been focused on something else, far away somewhere.

Williams said, 'Nothing'll reverse that *coup* now, Gran. If anyone was going to intervene –'

'*Don't,*' Jones broke in.

'Don't what, old man?'

'Don't wanna hear.'

Williams stared at him. 'What I'm trying to say is,' he resumed, 'if anyone was going to intervene it'd be this lot here. They're sitting on their hands. I've run the bare facts, that's all. Change of government, as announced. Hatim and Al-Bakr in charge, with the old boy's approval. Nothing about his being wounded. No republican propaganda, of course – we've been given the line from the Ministry, that's the point. I mayn't even lead with it. Only run seven inches. Above the fold, though, naturally. You want to see a copy?'

'No.' Jones's scowl momentarily attained focus.

Williams regarded him sadly: the grand old-timer Gran Jones so far gone. It was all one could say: sad. He could hardly make out how the old boy fitted together, crowded so awkwardly into the basket chair, jaw slack and the vague soggy eyes turning towards him sideways through half-closed lids, never looking at him properly – just hovering around his midriff or his knees like a cloud of midges. Sad. If anyone else had been present – anyone he could speak to – he'd have whispered, 'One day we'll all be like that.'

Jones suddenly said, 'Which Ministry?'

'Information.'

'Balls to the Ministry of Information.'

'Know what you mean, Gran,' Williams consoled.

'Means nothing. Means they're biding their time. Waiting for a proper policy.' How could Williams grasp it, straight off the *Wolverhampton Echo* to this censored apology of a news-sheet where the staff (such as they were) packed up and went home at six as if the universe stopped at six? Williams was a fool and had no cigarettes . . . though at least preferable to that rabble in the Darwish.

'I have no purpose,' he began clearly, and then halted. He was going to say, 'I have no purpose in going anywhere else.' He noticed how when drunk his mind would shape crisp, clean intentions, which his voice would not always choose to honour. What he wished to give expression to was that he felt settled here, in this cramped and dingy newsroom. At home. Mr Granville Jones, *at home*. On the desk beside him beyond the empty tonic bottles a spike impaled agency typewritten copy. His eyes drifted up to the great red capitals, ACCURACY FIRST LAST AND ALWAYS. An echo from the *Echo*. A Paki had succeeded Williams as editor there, he had told him.

It'd turned out such an arse-over-tit world. A world of all sorts of inconsequential fragments, a perpetual cascade of bits and bobs, jumbled, meaningless, a tumbling unstoppable confusion of hopes and horrors, the flailing, strutting puppets, wood and straw, Hitler, Musso, Stalin, Chiang, Mao ... and nobody, surely, pulling the wires, yet such terrible wrenchings, *drang, stürm*, for Man, *pour la destinée humaine, la mission civilisatrice*, historical inevitability. Mountains of skulls and seas of tears. The thousand-year Reich gone to rubble in half a dozen. All in the name of order, coherence, purpose, 'accuracy first last and always'. Some 'always'! Liz, always. The boys, always. Romy, always, for ever, *sub specie aeternitatis, saecula saeculorum*. That he should have ever credited it with any direction, any reckoning, any justice, any resolution! That he should have once striven so! So cared! So loved!

Romy, who was *she*? Had she led him here, a will-o'-the-wisp, dancing and ducking ahead of him, up those narrow wooden stairs where the black fellow and his grizzled skipper had humped him? Humped him and dumped him. A half-corpse. He hadn't wanted to let them go, those strange new sudden friends, so late in his life, though he knew he had no right to hold them from their sea. Then Williams took him over, and Williams's dingy newspaper premises were after all a species of haven, peculiar to his kind. He thought: I should be grateful, I was lucky to catch Williams still at his desk after moving my copy on the oil company telex, lucky to shake off the tail Al-Bakr or Hatim had put on me: they'd have prevented me filing, spirited me away somewhere, maybe knocked me around. They gave up too easy, these cheap young political dabblers.

Dingy Williams in his dingy newsroom. In their very dinginess, a terminal security. Here his argot is more or less understood, the remnants of what he could once do acknowledged, his remnants identified like bits of a once-famed ship wrecked at sea years ago, forgotten by all except the marine community: this was the *Gran Jones*, by God, a piece of bulkhead, look! – a spar, a knob from a cabin door. Can't piece her together now, nobody can – the sea has half of her already, more than half. This is mere jetsam. But Williams is in awe all the same – dingy, boozy Williams with his phoney boister, stock-in-trade Welshness, and his dingy cluttered newsroom with his staff gone home at six.

'Go home,' Jones said.

'Not at all, Gran. It's a pleasure.' Williams meant it.

'Go home,' Jones repeated sharply.

After another fifteen or twenty minutes there would be nothing anyone could do. 'They won't remake page one after the second edition's gone to bed. Not for this.' His fingers flapped the fragment on which the Emir had scribbled his message. Another fragment. A bit or bob. Portentous.

'Not at all,' Williams repeated, jaunty as ever, from the 'Sports' desk. It was a big night, old Gran Jones needing his help, over the hill or not. 'I'll see you through, Gran.'

Through to where? She had led him here, and this was the endplace. He had nowhere to go now, nowhere he wished to go, no home. Maybe he had never had a home, ranging the globe for news. 'Home is where your typewriter is.' That was what Liz used to say of him proudly when they were first married, and he quoted it to Romy the very first time they were in bed together, *Home is where my typewriter is.*

'Your typewriter is a professional disgrace.' Romy's voice, here, in his head. And dawn already stealing through the window of her bedroom in the Residency annexe. It's only the second morning after they first met at her father's dinner-table, such is the force and speed at which a love-line breaks upon a fate-line.

'I'm a descendant of Cain,' he murmurs to her beside him, 'a fugitive and a vagabond on the earth.'

She has her own information. 'He came to live in the land of Nod.'

'Who?'

'Oh, for heaven's sake – Cain. How can you not know that? Where were you at school?'

'We wrote on slates.'

She slips out of bed with a rustle of sheets to fetch the Bible, and there and then obliges him to read Genesis where it tells of Nod being 'east of Eden'. The Pentateuch is one of her archaeological sources. He has to take the Good Book over by the window to read it without his spectacles. Outside in the compound the lifeless British flag on its pole that frees slaves.

'Where exactly is Nod?'

'Exactly?' she echoes.

'Does anybody know?'

'Funnily enough, the site has recently been located.'

'Where?'

'Here.'

'No. Really?'

'Yes – *here*.' She is lifting the sheet to invite him back to bed and to herself. To Nod.

She whispers, 'Nod is Old Hebrew for "a place of exile".'

'What happened to Cain in the end?'

'He settled down and had a big family.'

Williams said, 'You could come home with me. The settee lets down.' He had never got so close to Fleet Street before. International newsmen never came to this place.

'I want to stay here, Williams, if you don't mind.'

Were the only fragments that counted the least preservable, like the utter surety and rightness after he had coupled with Romy, which were as utterly evanescent?

Williams got up and crossed to the disordered machine. The pomaded Indian still acted brisk and important; he began gabbling about the mechanism. Any fool could see the man could not reassemble it and have it transmit a picture to London all in ten minutes: he was still *extracting* parts. Jones had often seen such performances in the tropical world – a prolonged charade of professional activity, futile from the start, indeed the last state worse than the first.

'Have a drop more anaesthetic, old man. I get the best *sid* you can find.'

Jones disliked the taste but let Williams top him up again. Why not? It was apt, this kind of dereliction. A nest of newspapers. Tramps in England stuffed their boots with newspapers. Newspapers made tramps.

When his Arab friends had lifted him out of the taxi and into this back-street building he caught sight of the neon sign over the shop below – 'Al-Maimery': a curious name yet also containing its obscure aptness. A *maimery* for the destitute, the bust, the washed-up. An endplace for the ones with nothing to lose. Was this not the time that counted for most, when nothing was left for him?

For years and years now he had been shedding things. He who had had so much; the whole world. There was a time when the events of the world had no right to take place without his attending upon them.

Now, nothing. He said to himself: so it has come to this. A reporter without a pen. Powerless to transmit a simple image. Fumbling about in his mind he came on his voluminous manuscript, and recognised it instantly as a monstrous exercise in worthless egotism. He hoped Paul would put a match to it. Quite likely, if they had come looking for him, they would have searched the *majlis* and carried off his papers: such was the way of uniformed men in time of tension, to whom anything written in a language they knew not was evidence of conspiracy. Let them keep them. A mountain of words. Let some back-room Egyptian translator in Security wade through it all. Let that underpaid Gyppo hack be the only reader of his quarter-century's worth of labour. Such sacrifice, such hazard, such wisdom, such ephemerality. He used to be able to read tomorrow's world like a tablet on a mountainside: he was seldom wrong. He could read unreportable facts behind the reported news, he could read governments, read nations, read races. He could analyse with uncanny swiftness those polar demons – rich and poor, weak/strong, black/white, north/south, left/right – tearing at the soul of the planet's principal inhabitant: knew them like players in a travelling troupe with their masques to perform. He knew the passion of men for identity – *their* place, *their* lingo, *their* God – and for what they thought they possessed or deserved. For such figments men would clamour, hate, rip one another apart, devastate, annihilate. In the name of their illusory claims to full humanity men would become beasts. He could read it all. So what?

Men would, of course, be gods ... but where God was, *nothing* was. He was vaguely familiar with that tag or text and though he had given himself no practice at this God of the wastes who called to him from towers, he saw now that his life had been an elaborate exercise in becoming nothing and that this might, just *might*, be a species of inestimable gain – the will-o'-the-wisp entrapped – as if for this ultimate distillation he had been spared. He could bring this paradox to the Emir: his old blood-brother whose entire authority was reduced to a scrap of writing so tiny it could be concealed in the palm of a hand where the love-line burst across the fate-line.

Williams studied his watch. Gran Jones seemed to him to have dropped off, his head lolling. Was this the sharp end of the profession after all, the way the big news really broke? He saw the thick hands, mottled with prickly heat, twitch momentarily and the Emir's paper flutter to the floor like a dead leaf.

Something was still to be resolved, Jones knew. A bird flapping and fluttering. They made the holy spirit a dove, but this was his parrot troubling him. His parrot would die if Aziz neglected to call in and feed it. The parrot was the residual duty impeding his attainment of nothing in this endplace newsroom. The parrot tethered him and would not allow him to go, like a stick caught on a stream-bed vibrating against the current. The bird struggling and the stick trembling snagged his release – for he was otherwise ready now to let go, to abandon himself, to become so naked as to shed body also ... shed everything except a necessary *stupor* concerning wherever he would be borne away.

Through half-closed eyes he saw the Indian mechanic beginning to reassemble the wirephoto machine and he was aware that his grey parrot with the red feathers in its tail was of an importance that still forbade him to be gone. The red tail feathers, he knew, were a symbol of good fortune: just as the life of the bird must be preserved for a vehicle of providence in its tail feathers, so he must not let go because of his fragment of truth. It was somewhere about his person, a truth, a purity amid all the chicanery and confusion and worthlessness: a crumple of paper among the ants, the last footstep in the lone sands.

Williams said, 'I think we're getting somewhere, Gran.'

Truth was indivisible, he was well aware. A gem purity.

Williams got up from 'Sports' and went over to the mechanic with his clean photostat of the Emir's message. Then he crossed to where Jones was slumped in his basket chair, picked up the original where it had drifted to the floor and slipped it between Jones's finger and thumb. Jones stirred and peered at his watch but couldn't focus. Normally he filled his parrot's trough with seed before going to bed.

The mechanic worked on, reassembling.

'How d'you come by the name Granville? It's not Welsh at all – Granville.'

A question. A question to answer.

'I was christened Geraint.'

'That's Welsh enough!' Williams exclaimed. 'Why didn't you stick with it, for heaven's sake?'

'I'm not Welsh.'

'A name like Geraint, you're a Welshman!'

'I'm not Welsh,' Jones repeated sharply. 'Nobody knows how to pronounce Geraint.' It was an affectation of his father. They were a Shropshire family, English side of the dyke. As soon as he got to Fleet Street they advised him to drop it. Nobody had called him Geraint for years.

'How come Granville then?'

'My mother's name.' It had made her proud, his adopting her name. What he remembered were her fingers on his skin, soaping him in the upstairs bath.

'You should have stuck with Geraint, boyo,' Williams chuckled.

In the end – that was before the War – Jones changed it by deed poll, to obviate misunderstandings and accusations of duplicity by foreign officials trying to be obstructive. He was already famous.

The mechanic put the paper back on the tray and clipped the lid shut, all ready to be fed on to the roller.

Williams said rapidly, 'We're just about ready to go.'

'If I go,' Jones said clearly, 'could you arrange for someone to look after my parrot? I can't remember if you know my house.'

The mechanic switched on the power. A green light was on.

'Did you hear me?' Jones demanded.

Williams frowned. 'I don't honestly get across to the island much.'

Williams himself dialled the prefix for Britain and the number for the *Post* and when the connection was made the red light went on automatically. The Indian pressed the button to begin transmission. Nothing happened. He scowled at the machine, first from one side, then the other. He withdrew a small screwdriver from his shirt pocket and stood with it poised between delicate fingers as if about to prick the machine viciously into life. As Jones looked across vaguely from his chair, the red light went out.

The mechanic shook his head at the personal affront. He switched off and began to remove a side panel.

Williams demanded futilely what was wrong now.

'There is vault in the machine,' the Indian told him. 'A meghanigal vault.'

Williams unclipped the photostat from the drum. He asked the man if there was any point in going on with it.

'Repair is necessary,' was all he had to contribute.

Williams put the paper on the Sports Desk. He turned to Jones. 'We won't get your second edition now, Gran. I suppose that's it, then.' He felt so sad for him: the state he was in, how he would never have such a chance again.

Jones said nothing.

Williams could not tell if he was asleep. He continued gently, 'I'd like to take you home, Gran. If you'll just let me give you a hand down to the car.' He moved across and peered at him cautiously. 'You don't want to telex your office?'

One eye opened narrowly, with a gleam of malevolent distaste. 'Washer purposh of that? Leddum shtew.'

Williams straightened. 'I suppose that's it, then,' he said brightly. 'I'll take you home, then.'

But Jones seemed already gone off again. Once more Williams bent over him.

Jones woke with a spurt of ferocity. 'I'd rather shtay here.'

'I'm not sure our good friend here will beat the problem. Not tonight.'

The mechanic had already resumed dismantling the machine. 'Tomorrow,' he promised hopelessly. *'Insh'allah.'*

'If you don't mind, dear boy,' Jones said suavely, 'I'd rather

shtay here. I'll just lie down if I may.' He started to struggle
from his chair.

Williams reached out to steady him. He guided him through
to the washroom and stood beside while he passed water, then
back into the newsroom to his own cubicle, where a piece of
stained carpet covered the floor. He made a pillow for him out
of a pile of back numbers of his newspaper and the old man lay
down clumsily on the floor along the partition of the cubicle,
almost filling its length. Williams loosened his canvas shoes and
saw the scabs where the thorns had torn him. Beyond the
frosted-glass door on the other side of the newsroom the Indian
was putting tools meticulously into a holdall.

Williams stood. 'There wouldn't have been much of a chance
of changing anything on the island. Those bastards are there to
stay.' But Jones seemed to hear nothing. Williams locked up the
bottle of *siddiqi* in a drawer of his desk. 'I'll warn the night
watchman. You might give him a fright. Not that he stirs from
his bunk.' He could not make out if Jones was drunk or senile.

He left the door of his cubicle ajar and a light on over the
Sports Desk. 'Get some sleep, Gran,' he called, as he accompanied the mechanic down the stairs.

Get some sleep, Gran.

And if we hurry now – as hurry we must – to enter Jones's
sleeping mind, we find him transported back a quarter-century
to that very first interview with the Emir on his third day ever on
the island, and for reasons that belong to the preceding night,
he has entered the palace in immortal rapture. He has a
notebook open on his knee, but is not writing in it.

The two men are seated across the corner of the great
chandeliered chamber, newly finished (that same chamber
where, only yesterday, Hatim the son received the aged Jones in
unwanted audience).

And now the Emir is saying, 'You appear to have learned
very much about our country during a short visit, Mr Jonas.'
The Emir's Arab accent is throaty and strong.

'It's an impression we like to give,' Jones tells him. 'Ours is a
grasshopper profession.'

'Grasshopper?' The Emir smiles and makes a hopping motion with his hand.

'Grasshopper . . . butterfly . . . Sir Geoffrey Burton has briefed me well. Miss Romy has driven me around. Including to her archaeological site.'

'Ah, yes. Miss Romy is giving us a long history.' A marked rapport has flowered between the two men, even in this brief hour or so of their first meeting. In this, Romy has played a critical part – that she should have accepted Jones, she who to the Emir was everything pure, deep-trusting; for he has known her since she was a child and saw her slip quietly into the place her mother left, succouring the Wazir with the clear wisdom of childhood. The Emir has learned of this acceptance of Jones from the tone of his voice as he spoke of her, for he has already brought her into their talk several times. But now the Emir introduces a jarring note. 'Please, Mr Jonas, to prevent the mistakes, I request to read what you write before you will send it to your newspaper.'

'I feared Your Highness was going to ask such a thing.'

'Thair-fore?' All at once Jones perceives the Emir is an old man; he is only assuming middle age in a mutual pretence that Jones is a newcomer, for the sake of this re-enactment.

'Therefore I would prefer that you trusted me,' Jones replies.

'This is our country, Mr Jonas,' the Emir returns sharply, though this sharpness, too, is put on. 'Usually, I do not receive journalists. We do not permit the journalists to make the visits.'

'I'm honoured that you should see me, Highness.' Jones counters his bluff with courtly charm. 'It will help me write the truth about your country.'

The Emir regards him haughtily.

'I have been a newspaper reporter all my life,' Jones resumes. 'I don't remember a time when I was not a newspaper reporter. It's the only thing I know how to do. I grew up in the old school and the old school in Fleet Street where our newspapers are printed has a saying, "Facts are sacred."'

'Sacred?'

'Holy.'

'Then you may show me what you write.'

'Supposing I show you my dispatch, Highness. You will read it, and you will say, "Mr Jones, you haven't written this and you haven't written that. There are important benefits I have brought to my people. On the other hand, you have written this and that which will not help my people." I have to say to you, "You have the task of capturing the love of your people, and I have the task of capturing the love of my readers." It's unlikely these tasks will match each other.'

The Emir makes a wry face. 'The love . . .'

It is the proper word, Jones knows. 'Certain countries,' he tells the Emir, 'have forbidden me to return, because I have written the truth and the truth has hurt.'

'"The pen is more strong than the sword." Correct, Mr Jonas?'

'And rumour and hearsay are more dangerous than the facts. Your enemies will write about your country whether they have access to the truth or not. They are not interested in the truth: they are interested in power.'

The Emir's knee has begun to jiggle up and down. 'The young Mr Fuad Al-Bakr,' he says suddenly, giving Jones a narrow look: 'What is your judgment?'

'I have not met him.'

'But you have heard.'

'He wants to be Emir, Your Highness.'

'And so?'

'He was born into the wrong family for that.'

Jones knows that at this first meeting he has struck just the right note. Henceforth, all that passes between them is infused with rapturous humour.

'Look at me carefully, Jonas.'

Jones looks.

'You will observe, my beard is not coloured.' It is quite white, Jones sees with surprise. 'You know' – the Emir strokes his jaw, where the old scar shows – 'for fifteen years this is the colour.'

'I would never have imagined, Highness.'

'You are lying, Jonas. You knew well it has been truly white for many years.'

Jones returns a look of exaggerated seriousness.

'But you have never informed your readers,' the Emir continues.

'I have not indeed.'

'But it is a fact, Jonas! Sacred – correct? So now I wish you to inform them. That for fifteen years it is this white. I do not wish any man to think that our trouble turned my beard to white. Perhaps I shall make it black again. I think not, however. Now is time to be an old man. Is it not time also for you?'

'I am well known to be extremely old,' Jones agrees, for all pretence is shed. 'It's my characteristic.'

'So I see, Jonas. Even two legs are no longer enough; you must have a third.' (Jones has acquired a walking-stick.) 'Even so, when you require to be a young man, you run about, you cross the sea, take the risks. Why?'

'I have to feed my parrot, Highness.'

Jones knows that the Emir finds his answer very witty. They are full of devotion for one another and there is great joy in their ancient comradeship that Romy Burton has blessed. Yet only the slightest of smiles lights his friend's beaked face.

'Your parrot? Is that what old men require to do – to feed the parrot? I must make a note.' The suppressed hilarity persists. 'Soon, before long, I shall retire. When my son is married, I think, then I will begin to "feed the parrot".'

'Which son?' Jones is suddenly curious.

'My son Hatim. Tomorrow I will announce his appointment as Heir Apparent. The boy needs experience. The ulema have agreed. You may send this decision to your newspaper today. I do not expect the people in England, in the West, to understand. Perhaps you can make an explanation for them. "The Red Prince" I believe they named him in certain newspapers. It is their privilege. It is also the privilege of the young to change from colour to colour ... Now, Jonas. We old men have few desires. I ask you: you wish to remain here on our island?'

'Your Highness permitting.'

'It is permitted. And your house – does it satisfy?'

'Yes.'

'There will be repair. Our contractor will visit you. I have been speaking to your neighbour, Suleiman bin Abdullah. He

117

has arranged that you shall not pay the rent. The rent is finished, *khalas*! Moreover, you also have sons? Two, three?'

'I do not deserve,' Jones says. But the Emir's face has begun to shine, indeed the whole chamber seems transfigured and to hold promise of overwhelming love. 'I do not deserve, I do not deserve,' Jones can hear himself repeating.

8

As Jones dreamed that night in Williams's cubicle, Sandy McCulloch and Lou Rivers are at work by torchlight on the premises of another small newspaper, that which McCulloch edits on the island across the straits. The machine which occupies them is identical to that which the Indian mechanic has repeatedly dismantled and reassembled in Williams's newsroom on the mainland.

The two men converse in whispers, and as little as possible, for they can hear from a floor above them the erratic sounds and spurts of chatter of the detachment of soldiery that the usurpers have detailed to garrison the newspaper's office. McCulloch, for his part, is doing this against his better judgment, for as he has pointed out, what is the value to any of Associated Press's client newspapers of a piece of facsimile Arabic handwriting with a caption giving a translation and adding merely that 'supporters of the deposed Emir are claiming that the message is genuine'? McCulloch has only consented to this escapade because he feels himself protected, by association, by the fame of 'The World This Week' and the ultimate inviolability of the British media.

He switches on. 'Let's have it, then, Lou.'

Rivers hands across his photostat. McCulloch fits it over the drum of the machine and dials the 14-digit number. He presses the button: instantly the drum begins to revolve.

McCulloch throws a plastic typewriter cover over the machine to muffle its humming and regular clicking. He glances at Rivers and catches his grin. Rivers whispers, 'That'll take the smile off young Prince Hatim and his funny friend.'

'AP may push it out,' McCulloch replies, 'but what newspaper will treat it as significant?'

'Look, Sandy,' Rivers says, so close that McCulloch gets a whiff of his excitation, 'when I went into this business, someone told me: If they give you a sheet of ruled paper, write the other way.'

Upstairs, a sudden burst of laughter, then violent clumping.

Dreams, it is said, even those of great complexity and extended narrative and prescience too, occur in a trice. By the same token, relatively tiny occurrences bear within them a whole train of preceding events and consequences. The occurrence later that night in Williams's newsroom, in whose editor's cubicle Jones lay prone, was in itself tiny – nothing more than the telex machine coming spontaneously to life, as telex machines do, and issuing forth on its roller a message of less than twenty words:

ATTN GRANVILLE JONES

CONGRATS SUPERB EXCLUSIVE. PAGE ONE LEAD 25 INCHES PLUS PHOTO OF EMIR'S MESSAGE RECEIVED VIA AGENCY.

REGARDS EDITOR

Jones would have guessed the events it implied. It meant that through the deceit of Suleiman and his son a copy of the Emir's repudiation had reached the whipper-snappers and one of them had succeeded in transmitting it to a news agency, which had in turn disseminated it to clients. And in the *Post*'s newsroom quite late that night – between the second and third editions – the Night News Editor would have telephoned the Editor at home or at dinner somewhere and the decision would have been rapidly taken to remake page one for the last two print runs, the big ones. The Chief Sub would have whipped Jones's copy, already set, off its spike and redrawn the front page on a layout sheet with a wax pencil with remarkable swiftness – thirty seconds or so – making a double column space for his facsimile handwritten Arabic message. For none of the opposition would have old Jones's story: it was too late for them to catch up now: with the Emir's message as authentication, it was a major *Post* exclusive. And it would immediately affect the interpretation of the coup in the major Western capitals.

Could Jones *actually* have known of this? There are certain clues.

The old man must have stirred in his sleep that night, perhaps feeling cold from the air-conditioning. For he pulled out copies of Williams's newspaper from the little heap that formed his pillow, and awkwardly distributed them over his legs and body.

There is the following further evidence, however, that he woke fully.

At the dawn call to prayer, the night-watchman stirred himself. Williams had warned him the previous evening of the Inglisi asleep upstairs. He entered the little newsroom quietly and saw beyond the door into Williams's cubicle the feet in their loosened shoes and the scabbed ankles. The watchman put his head round this door, and there he was, an old man nested among newspapers up to his face. He attempts to rouse him with a cough, for he would bring him sweet tea. The head is tilted away but the eyes begin to tell him, since they are open, and perhaps open on nothing. When he lifts one of the Inglisi's long legs and it resists with the resistance not of will but of matter, he cannot doubt further: the intrusion here upon his premises is more than that of an old stranger and the sleep longer than any night's. Then he sees the brief telex message, already quoted, *gripped in the dead man's mottled hand*. The thought occurs to him, Could it have been bad news that killed him?

The following morning – that is, the Tuesday – Carew of Reuters crossed the foyer of the Darwish Hotel carrying a copy of the *Morning Post*, dated the previous day and just flown in from London. Guests conferred excitedly in knots. No soldiers were in evidence now.

'Hey, Shaun!' It was Rivers accosting him, with Mick and Phil in attendance, loaded with their filming and sound recording gear. 'What's the latest?'

Carew frowned. It was time, he felt, for Rivers to gather some news on his own account instead of milking it from other journalists.

'Do I hear Al-Bakr's scarpered?'

'You do,' Carew confirmed.

'Is that safe?'

'It'll be all over the world's press by the time you go on the air. I thought you'd be out in the streets filming.'

'We're on our way. We're on our way.'

'The Emir's been driving around the town with Hatim beside him waving at the people.'

'With *Hatim*?'

Carew frowned again. 'You don't know much about the Arabs, Lou, do you?'

Rivers was stung. Then he spotted the copy of the *Post* in Carew's hand. 'D'you mind? Yesterday's?' He opened out the front page, which carried the headline GULF EMIR DEFIES USURPERS under a strap which read, 'Island Ruler Passes Message to *Morning Post* Correspondent.' Under the byline, and alongside the picture of the Emir's message, appeared a photograph of Granville Jones, taken a good thirty years ago, wearing a felt hat at a rakish angle. He was only just recognisable. Mick and Phil peered over Rivers's shoulder.

'The old devil!' Rivers exclaimed softly in genuine admiration.

But Carew enquired, 'Which one?'

'Old Gran.' Rivers chuckled. 'He swore to us the Emir never gave interviews! The old *devil*! How the hell did he move it?'

Carew said, 'That's what tipped it – that story of Gran's.' It was obvious. After that, Washington and London would withhold recognition. They were bound to. It meant all the neighbours would rally to the Emir. 'Hatim knew the game was up.'

Rivers handed back the newspaper and prepared to hasten out. He supposed, he said, the Emir would 'load Jones up with a sack or two of gold.'

Carew mocked him. 'A golden harp would be more appropriate.'

Rivers seemed puzzled.

'You didn't hear?' Carew said. 'He popped off. The night he filed.'

'The old devil!'

As Rivers hurried down the main steps of the Darwish into the ferocious sun, was there not in his eyes a certain reflectiveness never quite present before? For two or three descending steps, yes. Then the sunlight, and the roar of event.